THE RIDDLE
OF MYSTERY INN

THE RIDDLE OF MYSTERY INN

•

Kent Conwell

AVALON BOOKS
NEW YORK

PRINTED IN THE UNITED STATES OF AMERICA
ON ACID-FREE PAPER
BY HADDON CRAFTSMEN, BLOOMSBURG, PENNSYLVANIA

To my daughters, Susan and Amy, and to Gayle, my wife.
Thanks for always being there.

Chapter One

BJ Galloway didn't believe in ghosts or goblins. He didn't believe in zombies, banshees, or poltergeists. He believed in what he could see. He believed in hard, indisputable evidence, the kind that could not be twisted or manipulated even by the slickest of lawyers. As far as he was concerned, those intellectually challenged fanatics who believed in the paranormal were prime suckers for some slick salesman to hook them on a correspondence course in voodoo hoodoo.

But now here he was, no different than any other black magic groupie, standing before a silver chain draped across the doorway that opened into the sparely furnished efficiency apartment that Mystery Inn touted as haunted.

Glancing surreptitiously at his Significant Other beside him, he read the framed placard dangling from the chain.

TOUR HOURS: 8 A.M.–4 P.M.

In this room on June 24, 1997, Carl Graves was found murdered at his desk, stabbed in the back with a weapon that left a large round hole. Neither the murder weapon nor the perpetrator was ever discovered. The room was locked from the inside. Some say his ghost roams the halls of Mystery Inn, searching for his killer and protecting his hidden wealth.

"Is that supposed to be blood?" The striking woman at BJ's side, Teri Owens, pointed to the mannequin slumped over the kitchen table. From a hole in the back, a stream of red ran down the shirt to pool on the floor at his feet.

Galloway nodded. "I suppose." He glanced at the window in the far wall through which he saw the gently swaying limbs of a nearby tree. Spaced around the room, informational placards provided more detailed explanations.

Teri leaned across the chain and squinted at the card next to the window. She grumbled, "I wish they would let us inside. I can't read the other cards."

A garrulous voice behind them broke the silence. "Puzzling, isn't it? The windows and doors were locked. No way the killer could have escaped unless he could walk through walls—like a ghost."

Teri jerked back in surprise as Galloway turned to the voice.

A thin man, his face scarred by acne, stared at him. He was a couple of inches taller than Galloway's own five-foot-eleven. Galloway nodded to the room. "You know about it?"

The man nodded, his gaze flicking over Galloway's shoulder, then back over his own. "More than you think, Mister Galloway. More than I want to know."

Galloway glanced at Teri. "You have the advantage, pal."

Releasing a deep breath and glancing over his shoulder once again, the man grunted. "My name's George Sims." He nodded to the apartment. "The man murdered in there five years ago was my partner, Carl Graves. I'm afraid I'll end up like him. That's why I came to see you."

"Me?"

Sims glanced up and down the hall. He lowered his voice. "I heard you were staying here at the inn. I need to talk to you. I think there might be an attempt on my life."

Footsteps sounded on the stairs. Obviously frightened, Sims pushed past Galloway. He whispered over his shoulder as he hurried down the hall. "Later. Tonight. After the séance and the play."

A maid, loaded with fresh linens, rounded the corner.

Down the hall, George Sims shut the door to his room

behind him. Galloway glanced back at the click of the closed door, wondering if this was simply a gimmick by the inn to tantalize its clients.

George Sims hastily locked the door and then jammed a straight-back chair under the knob. He hurried to the windows, checking that they were locked. He glanced about the room, sweat beading on his forehead, his heart pounding in his chest. Maybe he should have gone to the police. But he had no hard proof. He cursed himself. Why had he ever picked up the phone? But then why not? The old maxim that ignorance is bliss appeared never more true than now.

He shook his head and closed his eyes. The timing couldn't have been any worse. With the division of his father's estate, he had the money to pay her off, and send her away—far away. Then a new start for Arlene and him.

If only he hadn't picked up the phone.

During the stage play that night, George Sims was killed when a stage-light batten fell on him, crushing his skull.

Early next morning with only the stars for light, Galloway stood on the covered balcony outside his room. The autumn air was warm and thick with moisture. He stared through the tall pines at the sea of canebrake in the distance, trying to make sense of the previous day's events. He rested his hands on the balcony railing and leaned forward, his eyes losing their focus and gazing into the night.

Galloway didn't believe in ghosts. Never had. He poked good-natured ridicule at those claiming to have witnessed a spook during a calling. He laughed at those who swore they had actually communicated with a spirit from the dead.

But, beginning with the cryptic conversation in the hall, the séance in the evening, and ending with the death of George Sims on stage, the last few hours had shaken his smug convictions, especially since the skeptical PI would have sworn Sims was murdered by someone or something that no one else had seen.

A soft thump sounded overhead. He glanced up at the dark

ceiling above his head. There came a second sound, like two pieces of wood squeaking. He turned and listened intently. Nothing. The only sounds were the wind in the pines and the intense hum of mosquitoes that had escaped the zapper.

With a shrug, he turned back to the railing, trying to pick up the train of thought the sounds had interrupted.

Behind him came the soft pad of bare feet. A warm hand touched his arm. "Can't sleep?"

He glanced over his shoulder. "Didn't mean to wake you. Sorry."

Teri Owens smiled brightly, her dark complexion made even darker by the dim light of early morning. "You didn't."

Galloway turned and put his arms around her. Her body against his stirred his blood. "These last twenty-four hours seem like two months."

She rested her cheek against his bare chest. After a few moments, she pulled back and looked up at him. "I've never seen anyone killed before."

Galloway drew a deep breath and remained silent.

She ran a slender finger along the bridge of his nose. "I love the crook in your nose," she said softly. "You never told me how you broke it."

He shrugged. "One of the perks of a PI." He chuckled.

Her voice remained a whisper. "You think he suffered?"

"Probably not. That steel bar with all those stage lights must weigh a thousand pounds. The poor guy probably never knew what hit him."

She shivered. "Such a horrible accident."

Galloway remained silent. *Accident?* he wondered. Maybe he was reading more into the events of the day than they actually meant, but when he added George Sims' brief but chilling visit in the hall to the figure he glimpsed on stage, or thought he glimpsed as the light batten fell, the total added up to more than an accident.

George Sims was murdered.

But, BJ Galloway was the only one who thought so.

He hadn't wanted to attend the séance the night before. He didn't even want to spend the weekend at the Mystery Inn

Bed and Breakfast, but Teri had begged and cajoled, and Galloway succumbed.

A successful businesswoman with five beauty salons, Teri Ann Owens had recently become enthralled with the supernatural, so when an opportunity arose to spend a few days at the Mystery Inn Bed and Breakfast on the banks of the Sabine River in southeast Texas, she lost no time convincing Galloway to accompany her.

The séance had begun just after dark, well ahead of curtain time. Eight or 10 individuals sat around a table in a darkened room, joined hands, and listened attentively as a psychic who gave a new meaning to the definition of corpulence implored the spirit of Carl Graves to manifest himself, to make himself heard or seen. From time to time, a pocket of cold air drifted over the table.

Despite occasional muffled exclamations from some of the participants, the recalcitrant spirit of the deceased never communicated with the psychic, a result that held no surprise for Galloway. Once or twice during the séance though, a throbbing pain struck him in the back below the shoulder blade. He shifted his position in the chair to ease the discomfort.

After the unsuccessful séance in which the spirit of Carl Graves had refused to respond, Galloway and Teri found the bar where they had time for a drink before curtain time for the play, a murder mystery in which the audience attempted to solve the crime.

Sitting at the bar, Teri looked at Galloway. "Well, what did you think about your first séance?"

He grinned sheepishly. "Not much. Looks like just a marketing gimmick for guests of the inn." He glanced around. "Is it?" He directed the question to the bartender behind the bar.

The fiftysomething bartender wearing a white blouse and a black skirt laughed. Her hair was in short, tight curls. She sniffed. "For the most part, it is, but there are some who don't think so. Some of Carl Graves' friends, so I hear, keep coming back to the séances."

Galloway frowned at the bartender. "Why?"

"Not that I believe it, but the theory is that spirits are more likely to return to familiar surroundings and friends. Of course," she added with a trace of sarcasm, "most of those friends are just waiting for him to reveal his secrets."

Galloway frowned. "What secrets?"

At that moment, a dining room waitress stepped behind the bar and began building two Tom Collins'. Unlike most of the employees, she wore a scowl on a weathered face that had seen more miles than it should.

The bartender stepped aside to give the waitress room. "The story goes that he hid a quarter of a million somewhere in this old house." She made a sweeping gesture with her hand. "They say his spirit roams the house at night making sure no one finds his money. Sometimes he makes his presence known by a puff of cold air or a flash of light like a tiny ball." She wiped down the bar. "Me, I figure the story is a crock, but then, I'm not too bright. I just tend bar."

Galloway and Teri laughed. He introduced themselves to the amiable bartender and ordered another Tom Collins for Teri, and straight bourbon for himself. The bartender built the drinks. "Nice to meet you, folks. I'm Myrtle Blevins. Folks call me Myrt."

At that moment, Teri gasped and shivered.

"Something wrong?" Galloway asked.

Eyes wide, she replied in disbelief. "I just felt a cold chill. Didn't you?"

He glanced at the bartender and shook his head. "No."

Myrt arched an eyebrow. In a light voice edged with cynicism, she said. "Like I said, some say that's a sign of spirits moving around."

Nodding in the direction of the séance room, Galloway spoke to Myrt. "You sound like you don't believe those things that go bump in the night are for real."

Teri elbowed him. "Of course they are."

Myrt patted one side of her short red hair. "Like I said, Buster—he's the owner—Buster uses the séance and play to keep customers coming back. It works. We have a lot of repeat customers here. Some of them come back just to hear the ghosts. Others dream of getting rich. Me, I don't know if the ghosts are real or not. As long as I keep my job here, I don't care."

Galloway frowned. *"Hear* the ghosts?"

"Yeah." She wiped at the bar. "Noises and strange sounds in the attic and about the inn." She gave them a conspiratorial grin.

Thirty minutes later, the stage-light batten crushed the skull of George Sims.

In the absence of Sheriff Terp Howard, Deputy Ernest Brocklin had carried out a brief, hurried investigation and grunted his satisfaction when the coroner pronounced the death an accident. Somehow, through an act of God, the deputy declared, the knot holding the rope slipped loose and caused the batten to fall.

As BJ Galloway rolled over on his side and draped an arm over Teri's bare shoulders, he reminded himself that one of his favorite principles was to keep his nose out of others' business.

Of course, he could counter with the argument that before the accident, George Sims had intended on hiring Galloway. Besides, Galloway had seen something on the stage last night. He just wasn't sure what it was.

His thoughts drifted. Suddenly, a soft thump overhead jerked him awake. He mumbled.

Teri snuggled closer to him. She giggled. "Better hold me tight. That might be the ghost of Carl Graves up there."

Chapter Two

Guests attending the Sunday morning brunch were somber, a mood hardly surprising after they had witnessed the horror of the previous night. In twos and threes, they huddled over small tables about the room, their faces dark and serious in contrast to the bright sunshine flowing through the expansive windows and French doors.

Galloway and Teri sat by a pair of the doors opening onto the broad balcony. She paused, her fork motionless in midair, staring at Galloway in wide-eyed surprise. "Murder?"

He shook his head. "Not so loud."

In a whisper, she replied, "Murder?"

Instead of replying to her question, he asked, "Last night when the batten fell. Did you see anyone near Sims?"

A tiny frown knit her brow. "On stage?"

"Yes."

She contemplated a moment. "No. There were two actors on the far side of the stage, but none around poor Mister Sims," she replied, popping a piece of French toast in her mouth. She paused. "Did you?"

Galloway sliced through his stack of syrup-drenched pancakes. He shook his head briefly. "It was dark, and the fake snow was falling, but I'd swear I saw someone or something shove Sims under the batten." Teri parted her lips, but Galloway held up his hand. "No, it wasn't my imagination. When we talked to Sims upstairs, he told us someone was trying to kill him. I—" He hesitated as Myrtle Blevins, the bartender, entered the dining room carrying a glass of grapefruit juice. On impulse, he waved her over. "Join us."

Myrt looked 10 years older in the bright light of day. Despite the cheery smile on her lips as she slid into a chair, Galloway saw the weariness in her eyes. "You look tired," he said.

She shrugged. "My relief didn't show up. I had to work late and come in early." She shook her head. "I'm getting too old to spend sixteen straight hours on my feet." She paused, a trace of concern replacing the weariness in her eyes. "You two doing all right this morning?"

Teri nodded and swallowed her food. "Still shocked by what happened. It was horrible."

The concern in Myrt's eyes turned to worry. "We all feel just terrible. It was a horrible accident. I'm just glad you folks are handling the incident all right. Some of our guests checked out last night."

Galloway spoke up. "Accidents happen. It was nobody's fault."

Teri shot him a puzzled look.

He continued. "Did you know him? Sims."

Myrt sipped her grapefruit juice. "Yes. He'd been coming here for years. Ever since Buster turned this into a bed and breakfast and claimed it was haunted."

"Buster?"

"Yeah. Buster Collins. I mentioned him to you last night. Remember? Cold fish. He turned this place into a bed and breakfast after Carl Graves was killed upstairs." She gestured toward the third floor with her grapefruit juice.

With a cynical laugh, Galloway quipped, "He can make twice the money now."

Teri shivered. "That's cold, Galloway. I don't think I could make money off someone being killed."

Myrt laughed. "I told you, honey, old Buster's a cold fish. He'll make money any way he can. That's a fact. And you'd be surprised how many come here on the outside chance they might spot a ghost."

"Have they?" Teri smiled.

Myrt shrugged. "Some claim they have. They say they've heard noises or felt a cold presence." She nodded to Teri. "Like you did last night. Personally, I think it's just their imagination."

Teri bristled. "You think I imagined the cold air last night?"

With a smile of appeasement, Myrt replied, "No."

Galloway chuckled and sipped his coffee. "Where did Sims fit in with Graves?"

"Oh, George and Carl were partners. Along with David Morgan. The three of them owned Continental Delivery." She shook her head and clicked her tongue. "Poor George. He took Carl's death hard."

Curious, Galloway continued to question her. "What about Morgan?"

"Beats me. I don't know him except when I see him. Talk I heard was that he didn't shed any tears for Carl. I don't know how he felt about George."

"What about enemies? Sims have any?"

She shrugged. "Naw, not that I know of. Only time I saw him upset was sometime back. He swore he was going to strangle his stockbroker."

"Stockbroker?"

"Yeah. I don't know what the problem was, but he was spitting nails when he came in. Downed a couple of straight bourbons, one right on top of the other."

Clearing her throat, Teri spoke up. "Did he act in a lot of the plays here?"

The older woman chuckled. She patted at her hair. "He must have been a frustrated actor. He was always in those plays." She sipped her juice. "It's a good thing he stayed in the trucking business. He would have starved as an actor. But to hear him tell it, they were only one step away from Hollywood. Why, he even videoed every performance and mailed copies to Hollywood producers."

Before Galloway could question her further, Teri changed the subject. "The séance last night. Was it really just a hook for us tourists?"

Myrt winked at Galloway, then smiled at Teri. "I don't

believe in that spook business, honey. Like I said last night, for us, it is a gimmick, a hook. But, some of them who was there last night believe it is the real thing." She paused thoughtfully, then nodded. "It's one thing to us, but as far as the psychic and some of them who were there were concerned, it was on the level."

Galloway leaned forward, curious. "Which ones?"

"Huh?"

"Last night at the séance. Which ones took it serious."

Myrt shrugged. "Beats me. I don't know who was there last night." She hesitated. "Wait a minute. I know one who probably was. Name's Jennifer. A small woman with dark hair. Walks with a limp. She's a temporary around here from time to time."

Galloway shook his head. "I didn't notice."

"I did," Teri replied. "Nice looking woman, about five-two or so. Had a bad limp. Wore a white pantsuit."

"Oh, that one," Galloway replied, a mischievous glint in his eye. "I remember her now. She had blue eyes, a tattoo on her wrist, and a tiny scar on her neck."

Both Teri and Myrt gaped at Galloway, stunned by his acute observations.

With feigned seriousness, he added, "And she graduated from Radcliffe."

Teri stammered. "H-how did you—"

Then she saw the grin on his face. "Why you," she exclaimed, aiming a harmless slap at his shoulder.

Laughing, Galloway ducked.

Myrt chuckled. "I don't know about that stuff, but that's her. Name's Jennifer, Jennifer Pelt. Seems like she's always at the séances."

"What do you know about her?"

"Not much. I don't have nothing to do with the temps. I've heard rumors though that her and George Sims had a thing going."

Galloway frowned. "Did Sims go to the séances?"

"Not that I know of."

"What about the psychic? She work for the inn?"

"Mama Marie?" She shook her head. "No. She's in town.

She comes out here on Wednesdays and Saturdays for the séances, but she has one of them astrology-type parlors in Lloydville for the suckers." She laughed.

"What about Sims' company, Continental Delivery? Is it here in Lloydville?"

"Nope. It's up in Towson. Not much of anything in Lloyd-ville. Most large companies are afraid of water down here. Lloydville's on a salt dome, so we don't flood, but sometimes we're cut off from the outside for a few days when the waters rise—just us and the snakes, and oh yes, the ghosts," she added with a grin.

Galloway chuckled.

Myrt glanced across the dining room. Abruptly her smile vanished. Galloway glanced in the direction she was looking. He spotted the scowling waitress from the night before.

Myrt drained her grapefruit juice and pushed back from the table. "Sorry to run, but I've got to get ready for the noon rush."

Teri and Galloway exchanged puzzled looks as Myrt hur-ried from the dining room after the waitress. Galloway shrugged as if to say 'who knows.'

Clearing her throat, Teri raised an eyebrow at Galloway. "You said you thought Sims was murdered, but you told her it was an accident. What made you change your mind?"

He gave her a lopsided grin and laid his hand on hers. "I didn't. I just don't want everyone to know what I'm think-ing."

Eyeing him carefully, she pursed her lips. "What about me?"

His grin grew wider. "You're not everyone. You're you. So, get your pretty little behind up and lets take a drive into the great metropolis of Lloydville."

She frowned. "What's in Lloydville?"

He shrugged. "Just say I'm curious."

At that moment, a balding man in wrinkled clothes stopped at their table. A sheen of perspiration glistened on his round cheeks. "Mister Galloway? BJ Galloway? The private inves-tigator?"

Galloway frowned up at him. "Yeah. So?"

Without waiting for an invitation, the man slid in at their table. "Excuse me for intruding, but my name is Buster Collins." He paused and drew a breath, at the same time massaging his chest over his heart. "I own this place. And I need help."

Arching an eyebrow, Galloway studied Buster Collins. He didn't look like a cold fish.

Chapter Three

Buster Collins' disheveled appearance belied his demeanor. He knew what he wanted and how to get it. He dabbed a handkerchief at the perspiration on his forehead and signaled for another pot of coffee. "I'll get right down to business." He slid his cup toward the waitress. "Just half a cup, Elisha."

Galloway recognized her as the waitress from the night before, the one Myrt had followed from the dining room only moments earlier. Obviously, nothing had improved the woman's temperament for she still wore her scowl. Collins gestured to Galloway's and Teri's cups and continued. "Look, BJ—" He hesitated. "Can I call you BJ?"

Galloway and Teri exchanged looks, his filled with resignation and hers with amusement. "Galloway will do," he replied.

Collins nodded enthusiastically. "I want to hire you, Galloway. I just learned that the sheriff arrested Mary Calvin for the murder of George Sims. I—" He closed his eyes and drew a deep breath. He looked from Teri back to Galloway. He spoke slowly in an effort to keep his voice calm. "Personally, I believe someone murdered George, but I know Mary can't be guilty. I'll pay you five thousand dollars to find the real killer." He dabbed at his forehead again, then tucked his handkerchief in his hip pocket.

Teri glanced at Galloway in surprise, but he showed no

reaction to Buster's belief that Sims was murdered. Galloway leaned forward. "Who is Mary Calvin?"

The waitress stepped back. "Will that be all, Mister Collins?"

"Yes, Elisha. Thank you." The overweight man nodded in the direction of the stage. "Mary Calvin is one of the cast members. Plays Sims' fickle lover. She's the one who kills him in the play."

Galloway studied the outwardly calm man, but Collins' rapid tapping fingers against the tabletop revealed his true nervousness. He continued. "Look, she's a sweet kid. Has a hard-working husband and two kids, a boy and a girl. He works at Continental Delivery. She couldn't kill anybody."

For several moments, Galloway studied Collins, sensing there was more the man had not revealed. "Five thousand because she's a sweet kid? That doesn't make sense. You want to hire me, tell me the truth."

Collins cast a harried glance at Teri. He leaned forward, speaking in a whisper. "All right, but, you've got to swear you'll never reveal what I'm going to tell you."

"Sorry," Galloway said, starting to rise. "I can't promise a thing until I know what it is."

"Okay, okay, wait." He placed his hand on Galloway's. "Please. Wait."

Galloway slid his hand from under Collins' and plopped back down in the chair. "So?"

Collins seemed to age 10 years in the blink of an eye. "She's my daughter. She doesn't know it. I don't want her to know it. Her mother ran off with her when she was a baby. No, that isn't right. I drove her away." He looked at them for understanding. "I wasn't a good man. I was in prison for a stretch. When I got out, I went straight. I searched years for her. When I found her, her mother had died. I was afraid to take a chance on telling her who I was. To her, I'm just the middle-aged old man who runs a hotel and restaurant. We're good friends. I even get to see my grandchildren at times. The little girl's a beauty, and the boy, well, he'll make a fine football player."

His eyes glazed, and he seemed to be drifting back in time.

"Where was she born?"

Collins blinked. "Born? Oh, a small town north of Fort Worth. Decatur. Thirty years ago."

"What was her mother's name? Maiden name."

"Derek. Chelsa Ann Derek."

Teri squeezed Galloway's hand as he replied. "Don't worry. Your secret is safe with us."

Collins eyes lit. "You're taking the job?"

"Yeah. I suppose I am." He glanced at Teri who wiped a tear from her eye. "All right. First, did the sheriff give any indication what evidence he had to initiate the arrest?"

"No." Collins shook his head. "Nothing at all. They said it was an accident last night. This morning, it's murder."

"Tell me about Mary Calvin."

"Not much to tell. Her and Frank were married about ten or so years ago. He works on the loading dock at Continental. She was a secretary out there until the kids came along. She quit to raise them." He shrugged. "That's about it. Nice couple. Go to church regular. Neither one runs around. They just stay home with the kids."

Galloway pursed his lips. "Assuming she didn't do Sims, who had good reasons to see him dead?"

"I don't know for sure, but I can tell you that David Morgan has been putting pressure on me to sell out to him. You see, Continental Delivery holds the mortgage on my inn. That's both George Sims and David Morgan."

"How did they come to hold your mortgage? Why didn't you go through the bank?"

The round-faced man grunted. "Ex-con. Banks tend to shy away from them."

Galloway nodded. "Go on."

"Well, I believe now that George is dead, David Morgan will find some way to run me out. He can't do it legally, but he can figure some other way. Plant some coke in my place or something. I wouldn't put it past him."

Galloway pursed his lips. The plot was growing thicker. "Why would he do that?"

Collins pulled out a cigarette and touched a match to it.

He gestured about the dining room. "This place makes a bundle. For the last four years, he's tried to buy me out, but I've refused. I think the only reason he didn't try to pull something before was that his partner, George Sims, was an honest man."

Shaking his head, Galloway remarked. "You don't think much of the guy."

"He's slime. I've heard talk he brokers some coke and Ecstasy deals, but I got no proof. I don't want proof. I don't want anything to do with that kind of business. You end up dead too fast." He glanced about the dining room. "Especially out in this part of the woods."

At least, Galloway told himself, Collins was right about one thing. Dealing drugs, whether natural or synthetic, was as direct a route to the graveyard as Russian roulette with five loaded chambers.

Collins continued. "I've worked too hard to get where I am just so some sleazeball can come in and take it over. Besides, I want to leave something for my grandchildren."

"What about this Morgan? Could he have hired someone to kill Sims?"

Collins frowned. "I suppose, but I don't know why. They were fifty-fifty in the business, which is good so I hear. I suppose they had disagreements like all partners, but . . ." He shrugged. "I don't think so."

Galloway studied the now calm man across the table. "Anything else?"

"That's it." With a wry grin, he gestured to his wrinkled shirt. "Maybe you're wondering why I think George was murdered. I didn't sleep much last night. I didn't believe the accident business like the deputy first said, so after him and the doctor left, I raised the light batten and tied it back in place just like we always do." He shook his head. "There's absolutely no way that the rope could have slipped, Galloway. Someone deliberately untied it."

After a moment, Galloway said. "How do you know I'm the one for this job?"

"That's what kept me up half of the night. I made some

phone calls. You come highly recommended although I was warned you could be, ah, well, somewhat opinionated at times."

Galloway grinned. "I doubt if they put it like that. 'Pig-headed' probably. 'Somewhat opinionated' is a vernacular a little too sophisticated for the old boys I run with."

Collins shrugged. "I was just trying to be polite." He paused a moment. "Well? Five thousand sufficient?"

"Five thousand advance. I'll bill against it at seventy-five an hour plus expenses."

The waitress stopped at their table. "Can I get you anything else, Mister Collins?"

He shook his head. "No thank you, Elisha." He indicated the dishes on the table. "You can take these."

With a brief nod, she began gathering the cups and saucers.

Galloway looked up. The waitress appeared to be in her mid-thirties. Her shoulder-length hair was straight, and her black eyes seethed with suppressed anger.

"I'll leave a check at the desk for you," Collins said.

"Good. I heard that Sims videoed all the plays. I want to see the video, plus I need a list of everyone having anything to do with the play." He glanced at Teri. "We have a little visit to pay in Lloydville."

Pushing back from the table, Collins smiled briefly and extended his hand. "I'll have it for you when you get back."

Galloway rose. "Before we leave, I want to see the rope that holds the stage-light batten." He paused and turned to the waitress. "Did you see the play last night by any chance?"

Elisha looked up at Galloway. "You talking to me?"

Collins frowned at Galloway who nodded. "I figured some of you who work here might watch the plays."

She glanced at Collins and shook her head. In a curt voice, she replied, "Not me. I was working last night."

Every Sunday morning for the last 10 years, David Morgan sat by himself at the table in front of a breakfast of poached egg, toast, orange juice, and coffee. Instead of skimming the sports pages as usual, this morning he silently studied his poached egg and dry toast while planning how he could approach George Sims' widow about buying out her share of the Continental Delivery. If he moved quickly while she was still traumatized by her husband's untimely death, he might literally steal his partner's share of the business.

The telephone rang, startling him. He jumped and muttered a curse.

A guttural voice said. "Morgan? This is Garcia."

Morgan muttered a curse under his breath. He couldn't stand him. "What do you want, Garcia? I'm busy."

"I hear about Sims."

"So?"

With a trace of truculence, Garcia said, "So, I like to make sure nothing changes, that things would keep going like they are."

Morgan narrowed his eyes at the contentiousness in Garcia's tone. "That depends. Did you kill him?"

"What makes you ask something like that?"

"Maybe because George told me about the threat you made."

Garcia grew defensive. "I didn't mean nothing by that. Why should I kill him? That's like killing the golden goose. What about you? You got more reason than me to see him dead."

Sensing he had the upper hand, Morgan grunted, "Look, from what I heard, last night the sheriff's office said it was an accident. That's where they'll leave it. I haven't heard any different, but for your information, I didn't kill him. I had no reason. Business is good. Both businesses," he added.

Garcia paused. So Morgan had not heard that the charges were murder. He decided not to tell him, just like he decided not to tell him about the private investigator Collins hired. Let him find out for himself. "Yeah. Both businesses." He hesitated. "Are they going to stay that way?"

Giving a long sigh, Morgan replied, "As far as I'm concerned, they will. Just don't get too big for your pants."

The stage was 25 feet wide with the rear curtain some 30 feet back. There were three side curtains on each side of the stage, all parallel with the proscenium curtain. The second side curtain draped against the pin rail, hiding it from view of the audience.

Collins pointed to the wood rail fastened firmly to the floor by iron legs. "This is the pin rail." He pulled a wooden pin from the rail. "The pins are removable, which allows us to vary the number of battens overhead." He inserted the pin in a hole and began wrapping the end of a rope over and around the pin and rail in a crisscross pattern while he explained the process. "Then we tie the rope to the pin rail by twisting it around the rail, around the pin, then back around the rail half-a-dozen or so times and finish off with a half-hitch around the pin. That secures the light batten. All the curtains and permanent props are tied to this rail."

"Which rope holds the light batten?"

Collins indicated the next to last pin at the end of the rail. "This one."

Galloway watched as Collins demonstrated the raising and lowering of the stage-light batten.

"So," Galloway said, studying the several twists of rope around the pin and the rail. "The only way for the batten to fall is if the pin is physically removed from the pin rail."

"And then it can't fall because the rope is still around the rail."

Pursing his lips, Galloway placed another pin in the pin rail. Taking a loose end of rope, he began winding it around the pin. "What if you twisted it around the pin several times without going around the rail? Would it hold the batten?" He pointed to the neatly wound rope about the pin.

Collins grunted. "Yeah. Wouldn't be safe, but it would hold it."

Galloway nodded. Stretching the rope taut above the pin, he slowly removed the pin. The neatly wound rope fell in a tangle to the floor.

Collins gaped at him, disbelief scribbled across his face. "Well, I'll be," he muttered. "So that's how it was done." Slowly the frown gave way to understanding. "Then all someone had to do was remove the pin, and the batten fell."

With a terse shake of his head, Galloway muttered, "And that's just about as deliberate and premeditated as it can get."

He glanced around, spotting a door near the first side curtain. "Where does that go?"

"To a hall. One way goes to the audience gallery. The other way is back to the restaurant and bar."

Galloway turned the knob and stepped into the hall. On the floor were two cigarette butts with lipstick on the filter. Using the tip of his knife blade, he picked them up and dropped them in his shirt pocket.

Chapter Four

Teri eyed Galloway with amusement as he maneuvered the Chevrolet Silverado out of the parking lot. "Couldn't resist, could you, BJ?"

Galloway shot her a dirty look. "You can drop the BJ business."

She leaned over and lightly dragged her fingernail over the crescent shaped scar on his cheek. "Oh, I don't know. I kind of like it. After all, it is kind of erotic to imagine being held by someone named Beverly Joe."

Galloway shook his head in mock frustration. From time to time, Teri got it in her lovely head to tease him about his name. "Just keep it up. My turn is coming."

"Oh, I don't know, Beverly. Maybe it will, and maybe it won't." Her eyes twinkled.

An only child, he was reared by a mother who had desperately wanted a daughter. Unable to have any more children, she named him Beverly, but at least she resisted the urge to put him in dresses.

The name was trauma enough from as early as he could remember—he fought one battle after another over the name. When his mother died, he went to live with his grandfather. The crusty old man immediately designated Galloway as BJ.

Galloway kept his eyes on the road. "My time will come. Don't worry."

Teri laughed again. "We'll see. Now, tell me, why are you

doing this? You have unfinished cases back in Houston. Remember? At least, that's what you told me when I was badgering you to bring me over here." She paused, a thoughtful smile on her lips. "Or is it maybe that you just couldn't refuse another puzzle?"

With a crooked grin, Galloway shrugged. "Always liked puzzles." He tapped a finger against the side of his head. "Keeps a man sharp. And a woman," he added, giving her a teasing look.

Tossing her brown hair from her eyes, Teri laughed. "I don't need any more puzzles. Five hair salons are enough." She looked down the road as it wound down into the swamps. "I hope Buster is right about his daughter."

"If she is his daughter."

Teri looked around in surprise. "What? You think—"

"One thing you learn early, dear lady, is that you never, never believe what you're told. You verify everything." He reached for the cell phone and punched in a number. "My secretary's voice mail," he said by way of explanation. "She'll run a check on the birth certificate."

After closing the cell phone, he nodded at the highway before them. "Maybe after we talk to this so-called psychic in Lloydville, we'll have a better idea of what we're facing."

Lloydville, population 131, had been through several booms and busts since it was established in the 1880s. First came the mineral waters and the tourists. After that, the loggers moved in, clear-cutting thousands of square miles of virgin timber. After the logging came the oil, and after the oil came nothing.

Now Lloydville had hitched its future on the haunted inn a few miles from town.

Mama Marie Devereaux's was not difficult to find. On the main road, sandwiched in among half-a-dozen bars, five convenience stores with gas pumps, a feed store, two mechanics, and two churches, was a bright yellow house with a red sign promising love, wealth, and a long life.

Galloway pointed it out. "There's the place."

Climbing from Galloway's two-year-old Silverado pickup, Teri straightened her blouse, making sure it was tucked in about her slender waist. She brushed at her cream-colored shorts. "You were planning on coming here even if Buster had not retained you." It was a statement, not a question.

He grinned and ignored her remark. "Gotta start somewhere."

"Are all private investigators as nosy as this? I mean, Sims didn't actually hire you."

Slipping into his linen sport coat, Galloway shrugged. "I know, but he would have." With a boyish grin, he added, "I was just nosy—no, say curious. Curious is a better word. I was just curious enough to wonder what kind of mess he'd gotten himself in." He laughed and winked at her as he took her elbow and led her up the sidewalk. "But now, our friend Buster has made it worth my while."

With a bright flash of her white teeth, Mama Marie met them at the door and ushered them into a candlelit room, the walls of which were covered by heavy drapes. Overhead, tiny stars twinkled on the ceiling. Her lyrical West Indian patois was a refreshing change from the east Texas twang. "Ah, my friends, you come to right place. This be the house of love and good fortune. Mama Marie, she bring you all the pleasures you dream of. You will be happy forever."

Had not Galloway interrupted her, she would have continued her pitch, but her cheery animation abruptly vanished when he said, "We are not here to buy anything. I want to talk to you about the séance last night."

With surprising agility for her size, Mama Marie spun to face Galloway, her ham-sized fists sunk into her ample hips. She eyed him warily. Her West Indian patois vanished, replaced with hip-hop. "You a cop, dude?"

A half-grin ticked up one side of his lips. "Nope. I'm just curious. That's all."

His reply didn't satisfy her. "What you up to? Writing some kind of expose or something? Newspaper man or one of them *National Enquirer* types?"

Galloway shook his head. "None of the above, Mama Marie. Ask my friend here," he said, hooking his thumb toward Teri. "She's a believer in all this—" He waved his finger about the room. "This ghost business."

Teri scolded him with her dark eyes. "Galloway! You don't have to be rude."

Mama Marie flashed a bright smile and slid back into her pitchman's jargon. "You be smart woman, lady." She jabbed a meaty finger at Galloway. "Too smart to be with this one."

With a laugh, Teri agreed. "I try, Mama, but you know how men are. But he is telling the truth. He isn't a cop or newsperson. He's just nosy—no, he prefers the word curious. Personally, you'd be doing me a favor if you'd tell him what he wants to know so we can go back to the inn and enjoy the rest of our stay." She glanced at her watch. "Which, I might add has only six hours to go."

Mama Marie reached out and with a sausage-sized finger touched Teri's cheek. With a rollicking laugh, she lapsed back into her patois. "For you, Cher, I talk to de man even if he don't believe." Her smile vanished when she looked at Galloway. "Now, what you want to know?"

The candlelight flickered softly, casting pale yellow ribbons of light over their faces. "From what I learned, you hold your séances every Wednesday and Saturday."

She nodded.

He continued. "All I am really interested in is your regulars. Those who show up five or six times a month."

Mama Marie frowned at Teri. "That all?"

Teri laughed. "I told you he didn't want much."

With a chuckle, the oversized woman replied, "That be easy answer. Nobody."

Galloway and Teri exchanged surprised looks. "No one?"

"Not like you say. Oh, they be some come, but not like you say."

Teri spoke up. "What about Jennifer Pelt, the little woman with a limp."

Mama Marie nodded emphatically. "I don't know de name, but they be one what limps. She come, maybe once a month. And they another one. She gots red hair. They say she work in de post office in Towson. They de only ones what comes regular like. Most of de others, they be staying at the inn. They just curious. Some even come by here the next day."

Galloway released a deep breath and gave Teri a weak smile. "Guess that's it." He fished in his pocket and pulled out a sawbuck. He pressed it into Mama Marie's hand. "Thanks, Mama. One more question. "Those two. Do they come to any séances other than those for Carl Graves?"

Her eyes widened in surprise. "Maybe you not be too dumb. Why you ask?"

"Curious."

"It be them two women. The one that limps and the one with red hair. They only come when I try to reach de spirit of Carl Graves. No other time."

Galloway vaguely remembered the two women. "They were there last night."

Teri stared at Galloway. "Why do you think they only come to those séances?"

Several random pieces of information smoothly clicked together in Galloway's mind. He gave her a crooked grin. "Can't you guess?"

A block down the road from Mama Marie's, Galloway pulled into Cooper's Come and Go convenience store parking lot and went inside.

He paid for a six-pack of Budweiser and asked for the telephone directory. Lloydville and Towson were in the same telephone directory. It contained the numbers of five small communities. He found Jennifer Pelt's address in Towson.

Back in the car, he popped the caps on two beers, and headed for Towson.

The narrow macadam road between Lloydville and Towson dropped off the salt dome and onto the flood plain and swamps of the Sabine River. Stunted oak, tangled ironwood, and tall cypress lined the tortuous road, which was only inches above still water that glistened like brown glass. Often, heavy rains upriver pushed the swamp waters over the road.

Two miles from Towson, the road climbed out of the flood plain into the tall pines.

Arching an eyebrow, Teri glanced at Galloway. His face

was a mask of intense concentration. "Now, what was it I couldn't guess?"

He looked at her, then turned his eyes back to the road, a faint smile on his lips.

"Now what?"

Galloway looked at her. "What what?"

"That grin. I know that grin."

He chuckled and took a sip of beer. "I was just thinking how lucky you are to have me to keep you out of trouble."

She pressed her lips together and narrowed her eyes in mock anger. "Oh yeah? Well, for your information, I'm not the one leading us all over east Texas, visiting psychics and whatever you're taking us to now. You're the one who needs looking after. Not me."

And she was right, Galloway, told himself. After drifting along for five years after a nasty divorce, he met Teri at an American Legion Christmas bash. Her escort was inebriated by nine o'clock, staggering at 10, unable to walk by 11, and passed out on Galloway's table by midnight.

Bored by the party, and being without a date of his own, Galloway volunteered his help in taking her escort home.

They had seen each other regularly since that Christmas, both content with the easygoing, undemanding relationship between them.

More than once, Galloway had wondered what his life would be like married to Teri, just as he knew she, too, had wondered. But neither mentioned the subject, satisfied with what they shared.

"Well, are you going to tell me what's on that devious mind of yours or do I have to sit here and wonder?" Her eyes crinkled in amusement.

"To be honest, nothing profound. Just a vague idea." Without waiting for her to question him, Galloway continued "According to Myrt, Jennifer Pelt had a thing going with George Sims."

"Hey! What if Mary Calvin and Sims were foolin around?" She hesitated. "This could sure get juicy."

"Don't get carried away. Let's get back to the séance. The we can go wherever you want. Now, on the night Sims w

killed, Pelt attended the séance for Graves, which puts her at the scene."

"You think she is looking for Graves' money?"

"What other reason? Don't forget the second woman, the redhead who works at the Towson post office. Now, Myrt said that séances work better if those who attend knew the guy they're trying to reach. You're the ghost expert. Is that true?"

"I'm not an expert, but yes, that's what they say. Supposedly the spirit will feel more comfortable when it sees familiar faces around the table. Most séances have at least eight or ten people at the table.

Galloway suppressed his skepticism. "Why so many? Why not just one or two?"

"As I understand it, the energy of the group acts as a power source or battery by supplying the structure and medium needed by the spirit to make contact with this world."

The winding road made a sweeping curve into the city limits. Galloway pondered her reply. "How do you know if you've got the right guy—" He stifled a laugh. "I mean, spirit?"

She shot him a blistering look. "One way is if a séance participant experiences the same kind of pain by which the spirit died. Another—"

Galloway jerked his head around. "What did you say?"

She hesitated, surprised at the urgency in his voice. "I just said that at times, somebody in the séance will feel the kind of pain the spirit felt when it expired."

A cold chill ran down Galloway's spine as he remembered the sharp pain he experienced just below his shoulder blade during the séance, a pain in the exact location of the stab wound in the back of the mannequin sprawled over the table in the apartment.

He shivered. Impossible, he told himself. A coincidence. That's all.

Teri frowned when she saw the perplexed expression on Galloway's face. "Galloway. What's wrong?"

They flashed past the city limits sign. Galloway backed off the gas. He shook his head, refusing to admit any possible

connection between the sharp pain in his back and the death of Carl Graves. "Nothing. Nothing. Just a thought."

"You sure? You look like you've seen a ghost."

Galloway grinned at the irony in her remark. "Not quite," he replied. "Not quite."

Chapter Five

Jennifer Pelt was not home.

"Sunday afternoon. I figured she'd be here," Galloway remarked as he slid into the seat and buckled his seat belt.

With a touch of sarcasm, Teri replied, "Not every one stays glued to the football games on Sunday afternoons."

With an injured look on his face, he replied, "You know how to hurt a guy."

She laughed and quickly leaned over and touched her lips to his. "I'm ready for another beer. What's next?"

"The redhead at the post office. We'll try the sheriff in the morning."

Leaning back, Teri took a sip of beer. With a hint of challenge in her voice, she asked, "How do you find the redhead? It's Sunday. Post office is closed."

"I'm a great detective. I can find anything."

"Yeah? Just how, Mister Detective?"

Galloway's eyes focused on the emerald cut diamond ring on her little finger. "Let me have your ring."

"What?" Instinctively, she jerked her hand back.

He started the pickup and pulled back on the street. He nodded to the next convenience store down the street. "I'll just tell them we found a ring at the séance last night. No one at the inn lost one. The only woman we haven't contacted was a red-haired lady someone said worked at the post office." Galloway grinned like a 10-year-old with a new puppy. "Simple."

With a sigh of exasperation, Teri set her can of beer in the container holder and removed the ring from her slender finger. She held it up between her thumb and forefinger. "You better not lose it. You're dead if you do. That's two carats and eight years of my life."

He drove to the next convenience store.

An older woman with gray-streaked hair greeted him.

He fished the ring from his pocket. "I need some help please, ma'am. We're looking for a woman who might have lost this ring at the Mystery Inn. Redheaded woman who works at the post office here in Towson. We checked with all the guests and none of them claimed it. One of the waiters mentioned that this lady might have attended a séance out there last night."

The older woman grinned, revealing a gap of missing molars on one side. "Folks still going to them séances out there, huh?"

Galloway nodded. "Still going."

She eyed the ring with envy. "You sure they didn't say a gray-haired old lady with some missing teeth, sonny? It's right pretty."

With a light chuckle, he replied, "Sorry. Got to be a redhead, although I personally prefer dignified streaks of gray to red any day."

She cackled. "You're sure full of it, boy."

He shrugged. "Far as I'm concerned, if this don't belong to the lady I'm looking for, I'll have to turn it into the sheriff."

Shaking her head in dismay, she said, "Terp? Sheriff Terp Howard? Why, son, he'll have that diamond on his girlfriend's finger before you get back in your car."

Surprised, Galloway stared at her. "Who did you say the sheriff was?"

She looked at him oddly. "Terp. Terp Howard. Been sheriff around here for the last eight or nine years. You know him?"

"Yeah," Galloway nodded, a grin on his face as he remembered those years back in Houston. "I know him. So, can you help me out with this ring business?"

"Sure." She pointed up the road. "You're looking for a God-fearing lady named Sarah Hoffpauir. Up there two streets and turn left. Lived here all her life." Before Galloway could question her, she continued, "Her husband got hisself killed in a logging accident when she was about twenty-five. Raised a girl all by herself. Never remarried, though she does sometimes go out with Roscoe Creel who teaches history over to the high school. She lives in a yellow house on the right two blocks after you make the turn. Drives an old red Chevrolet."

"Thanks. Suppose she's home?"

Pulling out a pack of Camels, she tapped the package, pulled one out with her lips, and touched a match to it. "Probably. She ain't one to gadabout much except for them trips out to the séance things." She shook her head. "Never could figure that out. Once a body's in the grave, it's there to stay."

Galloway wondered at her words, remembering the sharp pain below his shoulder blades during the séance.

Back in the pickup, Galloway gave Teri a big grin and returned her ring. "Well, we got lucky. Seems like the sheriff around here is Terp Howard."

"How's that lucky?"

"Terp and me go way back. We knew each other when he was on the force in Houston. We gave him the nickname Terp."

Teri arched an eyebrow. "I'm almost afraid to ask what it means."

Galloway turned the key in the ignition. "Terp loved to dance. We called him Terpsichore, but that sounded to much like a sissy, so the guys shortened it to Terp."

"And you think he might help us, huh?"

"I don't know about help, but at least he won't run us out of the county like some departments do PIs." He pulled onto the highway. "First chance, I need to drop by the sheriff's office."

* * *

Sarah Hoffpauir answered the door on the third knock. She frowned up at Galloway and Teri. "Yes."

He introduced them. "If you don't mind, we'd like to visit with you about last night's séance."

Her eyes narrowed warily. "What about it? I wasn't at the play, if that's what you are looking for."

"Not at all. This has nothing to do with the play. All I'm wondering is why you always attend the séances for Carl Graves, but none of the others. You and Jennifer Pelt. You do know Ms. Pelt?"

Surprised by the question, Sarah hesitated, puzzled, her brows knit. "Why—why, yes. I know Jennifer. Are you with the police?"

Galloway noted that she kept the screen door closed. "No. I'm a private investigator. I've been hired to look into the incident." He paused and took a step back to give her more space. "I figured I'd begin with the two individuals who go to all of the séances for Carl Graves. I'm just curious as to why you attend them. That's all." He glanced at Teri who nodded her agreement.

The slight woman studied them coolly, her eyes reflecting her indecision.

Galloway continued, "You must have known him."

Teri spoke up, her voice comforting and reassuring. "That's all we are looking for, Sarah. Why you and Ms. Pelt go to all the séances."

She studied him a moment longer. "I don't understand. What do the séances have to do with Sims?"

With a slight shrug, he replied, "It puts both of you at the scene."

The smaller woman studied them a moment longer. A glimmer of laughter filled her eyes, and she opened the screen. "Come in, and yes, I knew Carl Graves. In fact, we were having an affair before he was murdered."

The tastefully decorated cottage was neat and clean, everything in its place, the drapes and curtains freshly laundered and ironed. Even the magazines on the coffee table were arranged according to size. Sarah gestured to the couch. "Would you care for some coffee?"

Galloway declined.

Teri said, "I love your house. Did you decorate it yourself?"

Sarah beamed, a light pink blush coming to her pale cheeks. "Yes. Well, with the help of my daughter and three-year-old granddaughter," she said, pointing to the picture of a smiling husband and wife with a laughing girl between them.

Teri picked up the picture. "They're beautiful."

"Thank you. I think so." She sat primly in a wingback chair across the coffee table from the couch and folded her hands demurely in her lap. She flashed a warm smile at Teri. "Now, what can I tell you?"

Galloway laughed. "Well, Mrs. Hoffpauir, you dropped a bomb about the affair with Carl Graves. Maybe you can start there."

Her eyes twinkled. She looked directly into Galloway's eyes. "Call me Sarah. And truly, I don't guess it was an affair in the sense that either of us was cheating on a spouse. Neither of us was married at the time. We went together for a few years. We were going together when he was murdered." She hesitated. Her brow wrinkled momentarily. She drew a deep breath and continued. "I don't know where the relationship would have led. Probably nowhere. He had his lady friends. Before me, he went with a woman named Joyce Purghan." She sniffed. "She was older than Carl."

Galloway and Teri exchanged amused looks at the woman's catty remark. "She live around here?"

"Last I heard, she was selling real estate around Lufkin. Always tried to look twenty years younger than she was, but she never could pull it off. I don't know about now, but back then, she had trouble with alcohol. There were others before her, but I don't know who they were."

"Back to the séances, Sarah. Why did you go every time?"

She looked at Galloway as if he had lost his senses. "Why, because of the money. Carl hid a quarter of a million dollars somewhere in the inn. I keep thinking that some night, he'll tell us where."

Galloway gawked at her as if she were the one who had lost her senses. He looked at Teri who, to his amazement, was nodding her understanding. "And so far, he's revealed nothing," Teri said.

Sara nodded briefly. "We keep hoping."

"Whose money is it?"

She looked first at Galloway, then at Teri. "It was Carl's. He had no family, and his partners certainly don't need it." She grimaced. "I'm sorry. Poor George is dead. I should say, his remaining partner doesn't need it."

"That would be David Morgan?"

Surprised, she hesitated momentarily. "Yes, but—"

"Someone at the inn mentioned his name."

"Oh."

"This money. You say it belonged to Graves. Where did he get it? A quarter of a million in cash is a lot to be carrying around."

She shrugged. "All I know is he told me he hid it at the inn."

"What about Jennifer Pelt? Can you tell me about her?"

"Oh, yes." Sarah nodded emphatically, maintaining eye contact. Her hands remained folded in her lap. "Sometimes we go in the bar after the séance for a drink. We're friends. I wouldn't say real close or anything like that, but friends."

"What about last night?"

For a moment, she hesitated, then nodded. "Yes. Last night." Suddenly nervous, she glanced at Teri. "We had a drink, then afterward, we both went home."

"Neither of you stayed for the play?"

She ran her fingers through her hair. "My hair was ratty. I had to wash it. I, ah, I heard about George this morning on the TV. I tried to call Jennifer, but she wasn't home. I hope she's all right."

Galloway sensed something awry. "Why wouldn't she be?"

"Oh, no reason, no reason. She knew George. That's all I meant."

He felt Teri's eyes on him. She must have picked up on Sarah Hoffpauir's uneasiness. "Does Jennifer go to the séance for the same reason you do, for the money?"

With a wry grin, she nodded. "What other reason is there? George told her about Carl's money. That's how she learned about it. She and Geo—"

She hesitated, lowering her gaze to the floor.

The furtive look in her eyes told Galloway she had said more than she intended. "What else, Sarah?"

She glanced at Teri and then back to Galloway, her darting eyes reinforcing Galloway's hunch that she was attempting to hide something, and he knew what it was. "Were you going to tell us about Jennifer's and George's affair?"

Surprised, she looked at Teri, who nodded their awareness of the rumors.

With a sigh of resignation, she straightened her shoulders and looked them squarely in the eyes. "It isn't like I'm spreading gossip, but Jennifer and George were having an affair. Have been for off and on for the last six or seven years."

"Off and on?"

"George liked to spread himself around, if you know what I mean."

"But," Galloway said, "he always came back to Jennifer."

"Yes. Truth is, she was crazy about him." She shook her head. "Why George's wife, Arlene hasn't learned of it, I don't know. She's such a sweet woman. A saint to have put up with all she has from George. As far as I know, she might be well aware of the affair, but kept quiet just to keep her family together. But back to Jennifer. I haven't spoken with her since I heard the news. I'm worried about her." Her hands trembled.

Teri leaned forward and laid her hand on Sarah's. "She'll be fine, I'm sure."

The trembling woman nodded, her eyes expressing her gratitude. "I hope so."

"Someone told me Jennifer has a limp. What happened?"

"Oh, she broke her leg years ago. She worked in a circus.

She was an acrobat. She fell and shattered her leg below the knee. It took a lot of therapy before she could walk on it without a cane. Then she developed a rubber woman act where she closed herself into a suitcase."

Galloway grimaced. "Must be double-jointed."

Sarah Hoffpauir laughed. "At least. Why, I've seen her fold her elbows almost to the middle of her back."

Galloway leaned forward. "Are there any others who regularly attend the séances for Carl Graves?"

"No. Just Jennifer and me."

"Has he ever shown up at one of his séances?"

"Carl?"

Galloway nodded.

She glanced shyly at Teri. "A few times."

Frowning, Galloway asked, "How did he appear? I mean, how did you know it was Graves?"

She shifted uncomfortably. "Different ways. Cold air. Sometimes a little ball of light, other times just a presence. But we knew it was Carl."

Galloway remained silent.

She looked from one to the other. "What are you trying to find, Mister Galloway? Are you interested in the money? Or George?"

Remembering Sims' frightened remark in the hall concerning an attempt on his life, Galloway replied, "Sims' killer. But, I can't help wondering if there could be some connection between Sims' death and Graves' murder."

"I don't understand. How?"

He scratched his jaw thoughtfully. "I don't know yet. I suppose I'm hoping that if I ask enough questions, I'll stumble across something."

She cocked her head to the side. "What kind of questions?"

"Just questions. All kinds. For example, did Graves have any enemies? Maybe someone who could have profited from his death? Maybe Sims learned of it and was silenced."

The smile faded from her lips as she concentrated. "Carl never told me much about the business. He was the accountant for the company. He owed money—gambling debts—but he was paying it back. That was the only problem between us, his gambling. I truly believe he was addicted to it, but with me, he was really very much a gentleman."

"You think that's where he came up with the cash?"

"Probably."

"How well did you know George Sims?"

"Not well at all. I met him once or twice—his wife, Arlene, once at a company party. That's it."

"What about the other partner, David Morgan?"

"I never met him, but Carl hated him. The only way Carl got the loan to pay off his gambling debts was because George Sims insisted Morgan go along."

By now, Galloway was forming some definite opinions about Sims and Morgan. Puzzled, he said, "You're saying Graves borrowed money from Morgan and Sims to pay off his gambling debts."

"Not from Morgan and Sims directly. From Continental Delivery."

"His company."

Sarah nodded. "Yes."

Galloway felt Teri's eyes on him. "Having a company like that makes it very convenient."

Sarah Hoffpauir smiled.

"But you know, I wonder why he borrowed from Continental to pay off his debts if he had a quarter of a million stashed somewhere?"

A sad smile played over Sarah's lips. "Carl was like that. He said the money was for his old age. He wouldn't use it to pay off debts."

Back in the pickup, Galloway waited until they left Towson and were down in the swamps before he popped the cap on the last beer. "You have to be back tomorrow?" He glanced in the rearview mirror, noting, then dismissing the dark sedan pulling in behind them.

Teri frowned at him. "Why?"

"I was thinking about snooping around for a couple days. If you can't stay, I'll run you back to Houston tonight."

Her brown eyes studied him several moments. "I'd better

not. Sometime in the next couple of days, we're expecting the state inspector. I want to make sure my people have dotted their I's and crossed their T's."

Before Galloway could reply, the dark sedan shot up beside them and slammed into the pickup, trying to send it spinning off the narrow road into the swamp.

Chapter Six

Teri screamed and grabbed the dash.

Galloway cursed and slammed on the brakes as the front right tire slipped off the macadam and into the brown water of the swamp. "Hold on," he growled between clenched teeth, dropping his beer and clutching the steering wheel with both hands in an effort to keep the entire vehicle from swerving off the road.

"Don't worry about me," she yelled, jamming her beer in the container holder and clinging to the dash with one hand and the overhead grip with the other.

The black sedan jerked back onto the narrow road and slammed on the brakes. Galloway punched the accelerator. The 365 cubic inch V8 roared. Three hundred horsepower kicked in as the Silverado, half on the macadam, half in the water, leaped forward, its wide, 16-inch tires scrabbling for traction. Within seconds, the speedometer hit 75. Tires squealing, the pickup clung precariously to the twists and curves in the narrow road.

The black sedan gained on Galloway. He glanced in the side mirror, recognizing the vehicle as a Lincoln Towncar, an old one. "Come on," he whispered, keeping one eye on the rapidly approaching Lincoln. "Come on up here."

Teri exclaimed, "What are you saying? Outrun him."

Galloway set his jaw. "Another few seconds."

"Another few seconds?"

"Don't worry," he muttered. "I got this sucker right where I want him."

"You what?"

The Lincoln shot up beside them. The black tint on the windows prevented Galloway from seeing its occupants. Abruptly, the dark sedan jerked toward Galloway. In the blink of an eye, he touched the brakes, backed away, then floorboarded the pickup, angling at the right rear fender of the Lincoln.

It was a defensive technique he had learned at driving school at the old air base near College Station. He had never used it, but now he would see if the training was worth the expense or not.

He struck the Lincoln's rear fender while the heavy vehicle was still turning to the right. The impact knocked the rear of the Lincoln forward, sending the heavy sedan spinning into the shallow waters of the swamp.

"Galloway! Look out!" Her fingers like claws, Teri clutched the dash, her eyes fixed on the road ahead.

Less than 50 yards ahead, a new Lexus rounded a curve, heading toward them. "I see it," he muttered, at the same time swerving back to his side of the road and slamming on the brakes. He glanced in his rearview in time to see the Lincoln shoot out of the swamp in a spray of mud and water and head in the opposite direction.

With a curse, Galloway slid to a halt at the edge of the macadam in the shallow water. He grimaced. By the time he turned around and got past the Lexus, the Lincoln would have vanished.

He climbed out on the highway and surveyed the side of his Silverado.

"How bad is it?" Teri leaned out the window.

The fender was creased and scratched. There were two or three crumples, but nowhere near the damage Galloway expected. In fact, the way his luck had been running, probably not enough to go above his deductible. "Well, I already had a few dings here and there. You might say those dings are now major dongs."

*   *   *

When they were back on the road, Teri leaned back in the seat and sipped her beer. She handed it to Galloway. Concern filled her eyes. "What do you think that was all about?"

He took a deep drink and passed the sweaty can back to her. "I was going to ask you the same thing. None of your salons caused some woman's hair to fall out, did they?"

"Be serious. Was it a mistake? Or were they after us?"

Ahead, Lloydville appeared through the cypress and canebrake. "I don't know," he replied, glancing at her. "There's a lot of white pickups out here. Maybe they made a mistake, or maybe they just wanted to see if we could swim."

Teri rolled her eyes.

Ten minutes later, Galloway knew the Lincoln Towncar had not made a mistake when he read the note scribbled in lipstick on the mirror in their bathroom.

> *Keep your nose out of bisiness*
> *that don't concern you.*

Galloway arched an eyebrow. "I guess we know who those bozos were after now, huh?"

Her face taut with concern, Teri said, "One thing for sure, they're not going to win any spelling bee."

A knock at the door startled them. Galloway laughed sheepishly. "Now they got me jumpy." He opened the door.

A young waiter in a crisp white jacket handed him an accordion folder containing a sheath of papers and the videotape. "Mister Collins sent these to you. He said to tell you the VCR is in the TV."

After the young man left, Galloway thumbed through the material in the folder. He glanced at the French doors opening to the covered balcony. The sunlight filtering through the curtains was turning to afternoon gold. He closed the folder. "Get packed. I'll take you home."

"What about that?" Teri gestured to the folder.

"I'll go through it when I get back."

With a soft laugh, Teri stood on her tiptoes and touched

her lips to his. "Well, I suppose then you might as well mix us a drink, open the folder, and let's see what's on that tape."

With an amused grin, Galloway said. "What about the state inspector?"

She shrugged. "Considering the bonus my managers get, they had best take care of it themselves." She nodded to the threat on the mirror. "Besides, nobody is going to tell me what to do."

Jennifer Pelt picked up the telephone on the third ring. She rolled her shoulders in an effort to allay the exhaustion creeping through her tired muscles. "Hello."

Sarah Hoffpauir's voice was urgent. "Jennifer, it's me. Are you all right?"

The small woman sat on the edge of the couch and shifted her twisted leg to ease the throbbing. Her voice trembled, feigning sorrow and distress. "Yes, as well as could be expected, I guess. It was such a shock."

"Oh, honey, I know, I know. I'm so sorry. Listen, do you need someone to talk to. I can come right over."

"Thanks, Sarah. You're an angel, but no. No, thanks. I took a Valium and it knocked me out. I just need some more rest, that's all."

"That explains why you didn't answer the phone or door this morning."

Instantly, Jennifer's senses grew alert. She kept her voice calm. "Oh?"

"Yes. I called as soon as I heard about George. Then not long ago, a man and woman stopped by. Seem like nice enough. He's some kind of detective. Not a cop or nothing. Asking a bunch of questions about the séances and George. He knows why we both go to Carl's séances. I didn't tell him, but he knew. He asked about last night. I told him we had a drink together in the bar and went home." She hesitated. "I hope you don't mind."

A faint smile played over Jennifer's lips. Matters couldn't have fit together any better than if she'd planned it all herself. "But, we didn't have a drink."

"I know, but . . . well . . ."

Jennifer spoke up. "I know what you mean. You're a sweetheart, Sarah. To tell the truth, I wanted to stay for the play, but I didn't feel too good. I left just after the séance. All I wanted to do was go home and get to bed."

Sarah frowned. When she left the bar the night before, she had seen Jennifer's white Pontiac in the back corner of the parking lot. At least, she would have sworn it was her friend's vehicle. She must have been mistaken. "You sure you don't need me to come over. You must be devastated about George."

The smile on her lips grew broader. "I am, but I'll manage. Honest. I just need some rest."

"Okay. Bye bye, hon. Need anything, let me know."

Jennifer Pelt replaced the receiver. For long seconds she studied it, curious about the detective. She couldn't help wondering just how far he was going to stick his nose in her business.

Maybe she should take steps to find out.

For the 10th time, Galloway replayed the fateful minutes of videotape.

The stage was in shadows signifying night. Snow fell gently. Sims' character stood motionless just above center stage, feet spread, his arm outstretched, gesturing to the two actors downstage.

"You can't see it?" Galloway shook his head in disbelief.

"No, I can't see it. Not the shadow," Teri replied. "It's all in your imagination. There's nothing there to see except that little flash of light—whatever it is." She hesitated and stared at him in disbelief. "You—you don't think . . ."

He looked around sharply, remembering the ball of light Sarah Hoffpauir claimed to be the spirit of Carl Graves. "No. No way. Probably a reflection of some sort off the stage lights. Now, watch close," Galloway whispered, leaning forward and placing the tip of his finger on the screen. "Here it is again. Right here on the back curtain, a shadow comes out and drifts to Sims—to that little flash of light. Then Sims lunges forward. Watch."

The still figures on the screen came to life.

Teri concentrated on the wispy shadow Galloway pointed out. She followed what she thought was the shadow as it moved across the stage. It merged with others that seemed to come and go in the dim light. Then the light flashed, and Sims lurched forward as the batten fell.

Galloway looked at her smugly. "You saw it then, huh?"

She shook her head, continuing to study the video. "No. But I think I did notice something that should prove to you that there is nothing to this shadow business."

He eyed her skeptically. "Oh? And just what was that?" A trace of amused skepticism edged his words.

Teri nodded to the screen. "The snow. There are no footprints in the snow when Sims stumbles under the batten. If, as you suggest, someone—the shadow—pushed him from behind, he'd leave tracks. So, where are they?"

Defensively, Galloway replied, "They were there. They had to be."

With a shrug, she suggested, "Play it back."

"You bet I will."

Teri was right. There were no footprints.

Chapter Seven

In addition to the video, Collins had sent a flyer touting the play and a brief publicity bio and file for each of the cast members and director.

Murder at Mystery Inn is an interactive entertainment in which the audience has the opportunity to question each of the suspects in order to determine the identity of the perpetrator of the murder of Jim Green. Each dinner guest will be provided a list of questions that they must answer from evidence elicited from the cast as a result of questions posed by the dinner guests. The guest or guests who identify the killer or the guest who has the most correct answers will be awarded a free weekend at Mystery Inn including free admission to the eight o'clock séance and if they are lucky, might even learn the location of $250,000 said to be hidden somewhere in Mystery Inn.

Teri arched an eyebrow. "Not bad marketing. Wonder if I could come up with something like that for my beauty salons."

Galloway grinned at her. "Hey, a free pedicure for the ugliest toes."

Teri shivered. "That's gross, Galloway. Even for you."

"At least, the cast was small," he said, spreading the manila folders on the bed. He opened the first. Inside was a biography of George Sims plus a standard release form absolving Mystery Inn from liability for injury incurred during the play. "Here's Sims. In real life—owner of the trucking company. In the play, he was Jim Green, June Lewis' newest lover."

"Fascinating," remarked Teri wryly.

"This next one is Don Shahan—real life, school teacher. In the play, he is Marc Mills, jealous lover."

Teri wrote his name on a pad. "Who are the others?"

Galloway opened the next folder. "Okay, here she is, Collins' alleged daughter, Mary Calvin, real life housewife. In the play, she's June Lewis, fickle lover. Then we have Eric Guidry and Michael McBride. One is a gambler, the other is a preacher in the play."

Teri whistled. "An eclectic collection."

He opened the last folder. Galloway held up a snapshot of a balding, sallow-faced man with sunken cheeks and prominent cheekbones. "And here is our director, Sean Ross." He passed the picture to Teri and reached for the director's biography. "Teaches drama and speech at Towson High School. Once played on Broadway in *Cats*."

"Makes you wonder what he's doing down here," Teri said, adding the director's name to the list.

Galloway took the list. "Our next step is to start interviewing."

Teri lay back on the bed. "Sounds boring." Her dark eyes glinted mischievously.

Galloway didn't have to be a detective to read the meaning in her eyes. He leaned forward and kissed her. "Detective work is boring. Most of the time," he added, kissing her again.

"Most of the time?" A sultry purr cloaked her words as her arms curled sinuously about his neck, and she added in a whisper, "Beverly."

"Most of the time," he muttered, his voice husky and soft.

The telephone receiver slipped out of Ola Mae Sims Wilkerson's hand when she picked it up. It clattered to the floor.

Holding her Vodka Collins above her head to keep from spilling it, she reached for the receiver with her free hand, but her chenille bathrobe caught on the corner of the end table and threatened to overturn it. Muttering a curse, she managed to retrieve the receiver. Angry, she yelled, "Hello!"

Her brother, Sydney, shouted back. "Christ, Ola Mae! Stop the screaming. What's wrong with you now?"

"Nothing!" she yelled. "Nothing." She lowered her voice. "Everything seems to be going wrong at the same time." She paused, waiting for his reply. When he didn't, she said, "Why'd you call me? Something wrong?"

"No. I'm coming over to see you. In fact, I'm pulling in your drive right now. We need to talk."

Ola Mae snugged her bathrobe about her thickening waist and eyed her younger brother as he stepped on the porch. Having reached the big five-zero a few months earlier, Sydney Sims fought it desperately, trying to hide 30 pounds behind tight slacks and vest. Still the preppy, he parted his shoulder-length blond hair in the middle.

"You should get your hair cut before the funeral, Syd. Fifty-year-olds don't wear hair down to their shoulders," she remarked, holding the door as he entered the foyer.

"Forget it," he said over his shoulder, weaving his way through the overly furnished living room into the kitchen where he sat at the table. "Got a drink? Or is that a stupid question?"

Ola Mae plopped down across the table. "Your leg isn't busted. You know where the booze is."

He glared at her. "True southern hospitality, sis."

"You don't like the water, don't drink it."

With a disgusted grunt, he mixed himself a vokda and Seven-Up. "Talked to Arlene since this morning?"

"No. David is helping her with the arrangements."

Syd leaned back against the sink and gulped a couple of swallows. "That should be our place. After all, George was our brother. Of course, you don't look like you're too torn up over it."

Ola Mae pulled the throat of her bathrobe together with one hand. "I don't see any tears in your eyes."

He arched an eyebrow. "I suppose not. Old George was a pain in the rear, but he was our brother."

"And the executor of the old man's estate. Or did you forget?"

Syd's ears burned. "I don't forget a thing. That's why I'm here. Sometime back I heard a rumor. I laughed it off at the time, but now—well, I don't know." He sat back down at the table, his eyes fixed on his sister's.

With an expression of disinterest, Old Mae said, "I suppose if I don't ask what you heard, you'll be here all afternoon. So, what did you hear, little brother?"

He ignored her sarcasm. "I heard you had been asking around for somebody to take care of our brother."

"Take care? What do you mean, take care?"

He shrugged his shoulders, obviously uncomfortable with the word. "Take care. You know, kill." He studied her, trying to discern her reaction to his remarks by the look in her eyes.

An amused smirk twisted her lips. "Kill? You mean George? You really believe I would get someone to kill my older brother?"

Syd shifted in his chair uncomfortably, embarrassed by the admonishment in her tone. "I didn't say that. But you were upset when George refused to contest the million our old man left to the cancer society."

Ola Mae snorted. "And why not? He gives us a measly quarter of a million, but he wants to give a whole million to charity. Sure I was upset. You should have been too. George could have done something about it." She jutted her jaw. "But not George. Oh, no. Not him."

Syd eyed her shrewdly. "Well, George is dead. You're the executrix now. You got what you wanted."

Her eyes grew narrow. "What we both wanted, little brother. Don't go getting religion on me. You want your share of that million just like me. Don't deny it. And don't go blaming me for George's death."

Intimidated by his older sister's tirade, Syd shook his head. "I'm just telling you what I heard."

Ola Mae shook her head wearily and took a long drink of her Vodka Collins. "Don't ever listen to dirty rumors, little brother. Remember the one that spread through town a couple of years back about you having an illegitimate child when the kid really belonged to the high school principal?" He nodded, and she continued. "Despite our arguments, we're family. We'll always be family. So, don't pay attention to any rumors, you hear?"

Syd grinned shyly. "Yeah, sis. I hear. I'm sorry."

"Don't be." She went around the table and gave him a sisterly kiss on the forehead. "You're my little brother, and I love you. Just remember. Now that George is gone, it's just you and me."

Ola Mae leaned against the doorjamb and sucked in a lungful of smoke as Syd drove away, wondering from whom he had heard the rumor. As with all rumors, it was half right, half wrong, and the other half pure imagination. But, she reminded herself, she had told him the truth, more or less. For sake of the family, it was best to drop it all, let it be buried with George.

Next morning, Galloway and Teri paid David Morgan a visit. They found him standing on the loading dock, his necktie hanging loose, his white shirt wrinkled, and his fists jammed into his hips.

"Is that him?" Teri whispered as she and Galloway peered through the cracked window onto the loading dock. She wrinkled her nose at the layer of dirt on the sill.

"Must be," Galloway said, pushing through the door onto the loading dock. The stench of diesel exhaust drifted across the docks, burning their nostrils. The clamor of racing engines, whining conveyors, and yelling voices forced Galloway to raise his voice. "He's the only one who doesn't look like he stepped right out of the woods."

Morgan motioned to the driver of a bobtail backing up to the dock. He held up his hands to halt the vehicle, then grabbed a clipboard from a computer workstation and barked sharp commands to the two or three workers nearby.

They raised the rear door of the bobtail and immediately began unloading stock while Morgan checked off each item.

Up and down the dock, men scurried about, pushing four-wheel dollies into long trailers and reappearing minutes later loaded with various goods. Conveyor belts stretched from other trailers to scattered unloading stations along the dock. While the entire operation appeared swift and efficient, the warehouse itself was in dire need of physical maintenance. Paint flaked from the interior of the great doors that rolled into a ceiling that was almost black from years of dust and grime. Many of the bumper pads were worn through to the steel supports.

Morgan looked up when Galloway and Teri stopped in front of him. A roll of fat over his belt stretched his pastel dress shirt so tight a button had popped off. He dragged the back of his hand across his sweaty forehead. "Yeah?"

"Mister Morgan. I'm BJ Galloway. This is Teri Owens. I'd like to talk to you about George Sims." Morgan glanced at Teri and frowned. Galloway could see the impatience in the man's eyes. "Won't take long. Just a couple of questions."

Glancing into the bobtail being unloaded, Morgan called out, "Eddie! Come here." A middle-aged man hurried over. "Check off the rest of this truck for me." The man nodded. Morgan moved a few steps away. "Hope you don't mind the noise. I like to keep an eye on things. They'll steal you blind if you're not careful."

"No problem." Galloway shook his head. "I've been hired by Buster Collins to look into the death of George Sims."

"Buster?" Morgan frowned. "What's he got to do with it?"

"Ask him. That's his business."

"You a cop?"

"No. Just a private investigator."

"I knew you weren't local. Why should I answer anything at all?"

Galloway chuckled. "Matter of courtesy, Mister Morgan. You've nothing to hide, so what does it matter?"

A crooked grin curled one side of his lips, which appeared to turn inside out when he smiled. He dragged his tongue over them until they glistened. "Yeah. You're right, Gallo-

way. I got nothing to hide. I didn't kill George. So, shoot."
Before Galloway could speak, Morgan added, "I heard it was
an accident at first. Then yesterday afternoon, I heard it was
murder. Who did it?"

Galloway shrugged. "All I know is that the sheriff arrested
someone. He hasn't talked to you yet?"

Morgan stiffened. His brow knit, and his eyes grew wary.
"Yesterday afternoon, but he didn't say he'd arrested anyone.
Who was it?"

Galloway caught a flash of apprehension in the paunchy
man's eyes. "Mary Calvin."

Morgan relaxed noticeably. He shook his head and muttered an amused curse. "Why the little—I didn't think she'd
do it."

Galloway glanced at Teri in surprise, then turned back to
the overweight man. "What do you mean, you didn't think
she would do it?"

With a shrug, Morgan explained. "Well, It just seems kinda
funny. Last month, about the middle of the month or so, one
of my employees and me was driving up when we saw
George and Mary come out of the warehouse. Just as we
climbed out of the pickup, she screamed at him and almost
slapped his head clean off."

"What did she say?"

"She told him he'd better not fire Frank—that's her husband. If he did, she'd kill him."

Galloway cursed to himself. "Mary Calvin said that?"

"Yeah. But, later, George laughed about it. I didn't give it
another thought. You know how women are." He grimaced
and shot a furtive glance at Teri. "Sorry, lady. I should have
said how some women are." A sly grin crossed his fat lips.
"Some of them say the first thing that comes to their minds,
present company excepted."

With a wry smile, Teri replied, "You're right, Mister Morgan. Women are bad about saying the first thing that comes
to their minds."

Her snide response flew over Morgan's head. "Yeah.
You're right about that. Anyway, George treated it just like
a joke."

"Where did he know her from?"

Morgan pointed to the floor at his feet. "Why here. She used to work here years ago. Her husband, Frank, still does. I was wondering if he was really sick when he called this morning to tell us he wouldn't be in." He grimaced. "That's still hard to believe, that Mary killed George. When I talked to Arlene—that's George's wife—the sheriff's office was saying it was an accident."

"Well, I'd say he found something that made him change his mind, wouldn't you?"

He shrugged glanced around the loading dock. "It appears like that. Anything else?"

"This employee who was with you when you witnessed the confrontation—he is around now?"

"Elton. Naw. He took off today to go fishing."

Galloway nodded. "Where were you Saturday night?"

"Business trip up to Shreveport. In fact, I talked to my wife that night about ten-thirty or eleven. I was at the Paramount Motel. They'll probably have the phone records if you don't believe me. I got back Sunday morning early. That's when I heard it was an accident."

"Tell me, how long were you and George partners with Carl Graves before he died?"

Morgan frowned. "Carl didn't die. He was murdered, but what does that have to do with George?"

"Can't tell. Might be a connection. Might not. Unless you don't want to answer."

"No. Makes no difference. We started the company about twelve or thirteen years ago. Carl was murdered—let's see, four, no, a little over five years ago. Never found out who did it." He pulled out a package of cigarettes and offered Galloway and Teri one. They declined. "It was weird."

Galloway arched an eyebrow. "Oh? How's that?"

"I saw him not thirty minutes before someone killed him. We had a delinquent account in Shreveport I wanted to take care of—called Wholesale Supplies. I went to his apartment and gave him the books. I went downstairs for a drink, and when I came back, the door was locked. When we busted it open, he was dead." He shook his head. "Wasn't long. Thirty minutes, maybe forty-five."

"I heard he owed the company some money. He pay it all back?"

He hesitated a moment. "Most of it. I could tell you that George and me had to absorb it, but that isn't the case. Carl had no family, no will. As partners, we recouped the debt from his estate and naturally the government got its share. George and I kept the company—"

A young man in jeans, T-shirt, and carrying a clipboard approached. He extended the clipboard. "Excuse me, Mister Morgan. We need your signature so the Dallas load can move out."

Impatiently, Morgan scribbled his name and turned back to Galloway. "Now, where was I?"

"You were saying how you and George ended up with the company."

He nodded emphatically. "Yeah, yeah. So, the truth is, we really came out ahead."

"I heard Carl was into gambling big time. Is that why he borrowed money, to pay off his debts?"

Morgan hesitated. He grimaced. "I really don't like talking bad about my friends even if they are dead."

"You're not. You're just giving me background that might lead to whoever murdered George Sims. For all we know, George might have been involved with the same ones as Graves."

"No. Not George," Morgan answered fast, too fast.

"Oh? Why not?"

His eye brows knit in suppressed anger. "He was a good man. He wouldn't get mixed up with any of that stuff."

Galloway played the innocent. "Oh, but for the last several years, didn't he have an affair with Jennifer Pelt?"

Morgan winced. "How—how'd you find out about that woman?"

Galloway chuckled. "You know how it goes, Morgan. When folks start talking about who's messing around with whoever, they tell everything. And sometimes they'll even make up juicy stories. All I'm trying to do is find out if

George Sims had any enemies, someone who either hated him or was scared enough of him to kill him."

With a growl, Morgan said, "If he did, I didn't know about it. Sure, George and me didn't see eye to eye on some things. No partners ever do, but we worked good together. He was a good man. Yeah, so he had a thing with that woman. That don't make him a bad guy. Everyone deserves at least one mistake."

"What mistake is that?"

"George told me that when he tried to break off with that Pelt woman, she demanded a payoff—a hundred thousand. If she didn't get it, she said she would tell his wife about their affair."

"Blackmail?"

"That's what they call it."

"Think she would have gone to his wife?"

Morgan sneered. "She's like most women." He glanced at Teri. "Present company excepted again."

Galloway glanced at Teri. The icy expression in her eyes revealed the disgust she felt for Morgan. "Back to Graves. You never said whether or not he borrowed the money to pay off his gambling debts."

Morgan hesitated. He glanced around and sidled forward. "Look. Carl did a lot of stuff. He was single, liked to party and gamble. He liked the horses. Delta Downs was his second home. Gambling was almost like a religion to him. Yeah, I suppose you could say some of the money he borrowed took care of gambling debts. Some of it took care of the fancy cars, and fancier women. There could've been a dozen broads out there after him, but if there were, I didn't know about them." He drew a deep breath and stared at Galloway.

"Rumors have it that Graves died after stashing a quarter million dollars somewhere at the inn. Do you think he did?"

Morgan rolled his eyes. "No way. Carl was desperate for money. No way he'd stick that much back."

Galloway figured he had gone as far as he could with Morgan, at least for the time being. He looked about the warehouse. "Nice operation you have. You go out of the state?"

"Louisiana-Shreveport, Baton Rouge, then over to Houston

and up to Dallas. We'—" He grimaced and shook his head. "I mean, George and me wanted to expand on to St. Louis. Now—I don't know."

A shrill bell echoed throughout the warehouse. Moments later, a voice called over the loudspeaker, "Mister Morgan. You have a telephone call."

Galloway extended his hand. "Thanks for your time, Mister Morgan. We won't keep you any longer."

Back in the lobby, Galloway excused himself and stepped into the restroom. He returned moments later. He whispered to Teri, "Go in the women's."

She looked up in surprise. "I don't have to."

"I don't care. I just want to know what it looks like in there."

"What's going on? You getting some kind of fetish?"

"Just do it."

She returned moments later. She shivered. "It's a good thing I didn't have to use it. Why—"

"It's a mess, right?" Galloway nodded.

She looked up at him in surprise. "How—yes, it's filthy. A couple of commodes are even broken."

Taking her elbow, he led her from the building. "That's what I figured."

Chapter Eight

Outside, they sat in the Silverado studying the rundown building. A row of steel casement windows just below the roof stretched around the metal building. Several of the windows had broken panes. Rust showed through the faded green paint on the sides of the building. Weeds grew through the cracks in the sidewalk, and potholes dotted the parking lot in which a dozen or so older model pickups and sedans were parked. Patches of Kudzu vines grew over the 10-foot-high chain-link fence surrounding the property. "It doesn't appear they spend much on keeping the building or grounds in shape.

"I noticed." Teri nodded to a new Viper in the parking space designated for David Morgan. "But it appears he certainly takes care of himself."

"Yeah." Galloway backed out and headed for the gate. "Makes you wonder, huh?" Back on the highway, he said, "What do you think about the guy?"

She considered the question a moment. "I think Buster Collins was pretty close with his assessment of the man. What did he call him—sleaze?"

"I think the operative word was slime."

She nodded. "I beg your pardon. Slime. Yeah, probably slime is a little more apt description."

Galloway pulled into the first convenience store and returned with a six-pack of Budweiser and the address for David Morgan.

"Why his address?" Teri sipped her beer.

"I'm curious."

She rolled her eyes. "Why doesn't that surprise me?"

"No. Think about it. Here he is, driving a seventy thousand dollar sports car while his building is falling down about his ears. Something doesn't fit."

"Maybe he's just one of those misguided jocks who have to have an expensive sports car to show off to the women."

Galloway agreed. "We'll see."

They saw.

David Morgan lived in the Golden Oaks Addition, a gated community 15 miles north of Towson where the least expensive mansion was half a million.

From outside the gate, Galloway watched Cadillacs, Mercedes', Jaguars, and a dozen other brands of luxurious vehicles pass in and out of the community.

"I don't know about you, missy," he drawled, "but I have a sneaky feeling that Mister Morgan's standard of living far exceeds his income from the trucking company."

"How much do you figure he makes?"

"I don't know, but his company is regional. Two partners. I don't see how they could pull down more than a hundred, maybe one-twenty-five a year."

"Is there any way to find out?"

Galloway turned up his beer and drained it. "Maybe Arlene Sims can tell us."

During the drive, Galloway bounced ideas off Teri. "You see how nervous he got when I told him the sheriff had arrested someone?"

"You noticed it too, huh? I thought it was just my imagination. He sure relaxed when you told him who it was."

"Yeah. Makes you wonder. Someone comes up to you and tells you the sheriff has arrested the one who killed a friend, you don't look around like you're trying to find a place to hide. You grin like the proverbial possum."

"Was it just me," Teri said, sipping her beer, "or did you notice that he didn't seem to care much for Jennifer Pelt?"

Galloway glanced at her. "You're catching on fast. I'd better be careful or you'll take over my business. Of course I don't know how you would advertise it. Maybe the Hairdressers' Skip Tracer Inc."

Teri laughed. "Oh no. I got my hands full."

"Yeah, I think we need to do a little more digging on Mister Morgan."

Arlene Sims lived in a modest home in a well-kept addition just outside of Towson. Hedges in need of trimming grew around the perimeter of the gray brick house. Large oil stains dotted the driveway. The front door was scuffed at the kick panel from years of coming and going.

It was, Galloway immediately recognized from where he was parked across the street, the sort of home he would have guessed for a successful partner in a business the size of Continental Delivery.

"I'll wait in the truck," Teri said, indicating her shorts. "I'd feel odd wearing these in where someone is in mourning."

Galloway squeezed her hand. "You surprise me at times, you know it?"

She giggled. "Come on, Galloway. Be honest. I surprise you all the time."

His eyes crinkled in amusement. "You do. All the time."

At that moment, a black limousine pulled up in the drive, and a man in a dark suit went to the door. Moments later, a woman and two twentysomethings emerged and climbed into the limousine.

"The funeral," Teri whispered as the car backed out and headed down the street. "I'm glad we weren't a few minutes earlier."

After the limousine departed, Galloway pulled back on the street. "We'll try tomorrow."

"Everyone will probably be at the funeral today."

Galloway looked at her. "Except Jennifer Pelt. Let's drop by and see her."

Teri's stomach growled. She laughed. "Somebody's hungry."

Galloway glanced at his watch. "It's almost two. Let's pick up a couple of hamburgers on the way."

Just before they reached Pelt's street, a white Pontiac pulled up to the stop sign. Galloway glanced at the driver, a dark-haired woman about forty or so. She glanced his way as she turned onto the main highway.

They parked in front of Pelt's bungalow.

Once again, she was not home.

"Maybe we can catch her tonight," Galloway muttered around the bite of hamburger he had resumed eating.

Teri sighed and licked the mustard from her fingers. "It's worth a try. Now what?"

"Look in the folder and find Mary Calvin's publicity biography. Where does she live?"

With her free hand, Teri riffled through the folder. "Here we are. Let's see. She has a husband and two kids, and they live in Lloydville."

Circling the block, Galloway pulled back onto the highway. "Let's give the husband a try. Maybe he can tell us something."

"Can't you ask the sheriff? You said you knew him."

Galloway dropped what was left of his hamburger in the bag and shook his head. "Usually, it's best to wait until after disclosure, but that sometimes takes a while. Right now, he's gathering evidence to turn over to the District Attorney. The DA's the one who recommends prosecution. Then the DA has to disclose what he has on her. Maybe if Terp has all he thinks he needs, he won't mind talking about it."

On the highway back to Lloydville, Galloway rehashed his earlier visit with David Morgan. He was too absorbed in replaying his interview to pay attention to the older pickup pull out of the parking lot at the Towson Bar and fall in behind him, where the narrow highway dropped down onto the flood plain and wound beneath the spreading oaks and black gum overhanging the road.

Without warning, a loud thud sounded on the roof of the pickup cab. They exchanged puzzled looks. Teri frowned. "What was that?"

Galloway glanced in the rearview. "Beats m—"

He caught his breath, cutting off his reply when he spotted a figure leaning from the window of a rusty Chevrolet pickup behind them and aiming what appeared to be a handgun.

Instinctively, he jerked the pickup to the right, then back to the left, at the same time slamming the accelerator to the floor. "Hang on," he shouted.

Teri glanced over her shoulder. "Not again," she cried out, grabbing for the safety bars.

"Keep your head down. They're shooting at us."

She threw herself down on the seat. "But why?"

The sudden burst of speed pulled them away from the pursuing pickup. Galloway swerved from one side of the road to the other. "We must have touched a sore spot with someone," he growled.

He peered ahead, remembering the straightaway beyond the curve. "Up there. Hold on." Galloway braked before a sweeping bend in the road, then accelerated as he entered the curve. As soon as he hit the straightaway beyond, he flipped the Silverado into neutral, slammed on the emergency brake, and spun the wheel to the left.

The pickup swapped ends. Without hesitation, he released the emergency, popped the truck into gear, and accelerated. Smoked billowed from the rear tires as they screamed for traction.

Just as the Chevrolet pickup whipped around the curve, Galloway shot forward directly toward the oncoming pickup in a deadly game of chicken.

He glanced down. Teri lay motionless, her face pressed into the back of the seat. "Stay down," he ordered her. He tightened his grip on the steering wheel.

The driver of the pickup gaped in disbelief at the Silverado hurtling toward him. He yelped and jerked his truck to the left seconds before the white pickup swept past. In the next second, his eyes bulged as a Greyhound Tour Bus rumbled around another bend in the road less than 50 yards distant.

With a cry of desperation, the frantic driver spun the wheel to the right, then back to the left, whipsawing the rear end of the pickup.

The Greyhound caught the left rear fender of the rusty pickup, ripping off the pipe bumper and covering the highway with broken glass.

The rear end of the pickup skidded left and right as the driver desperately fought for control.

Galloway braked to a sliding halt, and whipped around in a U-turn. The heavy tires of the Silverado spun in the muck of the muddy swamp, the momentum of the truck sending the rear end sliding sideways through the shallow water. He floorboarded the pickup. Sprays of mud and water arched 30 feet into the air.

Teri lurched upright. She clutched the safety bars until her knuckles were white. Her face was pale and taut.

"I'll get them this time," Galloway muttered as the Silverado roared back on the highway.

But, ahead, the lumbering Greyhound careened around the bend on the wrong side of the road. Galloway grimaced, hitting the brakes and sliding off the road into the swamp.

The Silverado threatened to bog, but he accelerated, tearing the powerful vehicle free of the clinging mud and leaves as the Greyhound swept past. Back on the road, he abruptly slammed on the brakes.

A twisted pipe bumper and broken glass littered the road, blocking his way.

Muttering a curse, Galloway pulled to the side of the narrow highway. By the time he'd tossed the bumper in the pickup bed and kicked the glass to the side of the road, he knew his quarry had vanished. He narrowed his eyes. His time was coming.

Chapter Nine

"Think it was the same ones who tried to run us off the road?" Teri asked.

Galloway kept his eyes on the road to Lloydville. "Has to be. The question is, who's turning them loose on us? What is it with Sims' murder that someone doesn't want us snooping around? And on top of that, how does Mary Calvin fit in the mix?"

"You think it could be coke or Ecstasy? Even amphetamines? Collins said he'd heard rumors that Morgan was brokering drug deals. Maybe Sims was part of it, and Mary Calvin . . ." She hesitated.

"Mary Calvin what?"

With a shrug, Teri ran her fingers through her short hair, which fell right back in place. "I don't know what. You're the detective. Detect."

Galloway laughed. "You're doing just fine for an amateur. Better than me because I don't have any idea either."

She sighed and leaned back against the seat. "Maybe her husband can us tell more."

Frank Calvin said Sheriff Howard had informed him a hearing was set for the next morning. "I hired an attorney, Jess Wilson. He said that's when we'll find out more." The distraught husband and father sagged back in the overstuffed chair and stared sadly at his two children playing in the middle of the floor.

"Other than the play, did your wife have any contact with George Sims?"

Calvin looked at him sharply, his eyes cold.

Galloway explained, "I'm not suggesting anything. Just an open question so I can get started somewhere."

"I still don't completely understand why you're here. Okay, so someone you refuse to name paid you to help us. Why would anyone want to do that?"

"They have their reasons."

Teri spoke up. "Maybe they just like you."

For several moments he remained silent, all the while his eyes fixed on Galloway's as if he were trying to read the thoughts in Galloway's head. A slow grin curled his lips and a glitter of understanding filled his eyes. "There's only one person, and I figured he was dead."

The remark puzzled Galloway. "Who?"

"Mary's old man. He ran out on them thirty years ago." He glanced at Teri, then turned his eyes back to Galloway. "I always wondered when he would show up."

Galloway tried not to show his surprise at Calvin's wild guess. He shook his head. "You're way off base there."

Ignoring Galloway's remark, Calvin chuckled. "I'll be . . . after all these years." He arched an eyebrow. "I don't suppose you'd tell me who he is?"

"You're pretty sure of yourself."

Giving his head a weary shake, Calvin said, "Who knows? Maybe I'm wrong. You see, neither of us have family. It's just us and the children. The friends we have who would help don't have the money to hire a detective, and if they did, they wouldn't keep it a secret." He paused. "Even if it is him, I don't want Mary to know. She's has enough to handle now." He glanced at Teri and nodded. With a look of resignation, he continued, "So, you want to know what contact she had with Sims? Nothing unusual. We both work for him. Well, she did. She was a secretary, but left when the kids came along. About ten years ago now."

"They must have had an amicable friendship," Galloway said. "They were both in the same play."

Calvin stiffened imperceptibly. "Yeah. A few weeks back, Mary decided to quit, but the director couldn't get anyone else for the part. She agreed to keep it until he could find someone."

"Why did she want out?"

With an indifferent shrug, Calvin replied, "She was just tired. She'd been doing the plays off and on the last few years. It was a break from housework. She deserved the time away from the kids and the house. Even fun gets tiresome after a spell, I suppose."

"And you took care of the kids while she was gone."

"Naturally. She'd do the same for me."

Galloway studied Frank Calvin. He sensed the man was telling the truth, as he knew it. "Did she ever threaten George Sims' life?"

Surprise, then anger filled Calvin's face. "I don't know where you got that, mister, but it's a lie. My wife would never, never threaten a soul."

Now, Galloway sensed, the man was telling the absolute truth.

Sean Ross squinted from the lighted stage into the darkened gallery. Behind him, a handful of young thespians paused in the middle of their rehearsal. "Who's out there?"

"BJ Galloway. Private investigator, Mister Ross. If you have time, I'd like to visit with you."

His reply was curt. "I've already spoken with the sheriff."

"I'm not here in that capacity, Mister Ross. A private individual hired me to do what I could to prove Mary Calvin's innocence."

Ross hesitated, glanced at his watch, then after a few seconds, nodded to his students. "Take ten, kids." Dressed in cutoffs, T-shirt, and sandals, the thin man hurried across the stage to the stairs, looking every bit like a frightened killdeer scooting across the marsh.

Ross seized Galloway's hand with a strong grip. He nodded

to Teri, whom Galloway introduced. His deep voice resonated with authority. "What can I do for you, Mister Galloway?" He grimaced. "I can't believe Mary was responsible. I was backstage with her and Don Shahan. I didn't see either of them near the pin rail." He nodded in the direction of town. "I told all this to the sheriff when he came out earlier today."

"I won't keep you long then. Tell me, how did your cast get along? I mean, any feuds, hard feelings, that sort of thing?"

Without hesitation, Ross replied, "No. We were like family for the most part. Oh, we had disagreements, but this little play was just an exercise in playland, not even a candidate for the straw-hat circuit. It was nothing for anyone to concern themselves."

"But didn't Sims send videos off to various producers."

Ross ran his hand over his bald scalp and sighed with resignation. "George was eaten up with himself. Thought he was John Barrymore reincarnated." He chuckled. "Poor George. He would have had trouble being a straight man for the Three Stooges, but he was harmless."

"I heard that Mary Calvin wanted out of the production."

"I don't know where you heard it, but that's right. Mary did come to me a few weeks ago asking for a replacement. Said she needed to spend more time at home. I told her as soon as I found someone."

"And she agreed?"

Ross smiled sadly. "To use an old theatrical expression, Mary was a trouper. She did whatever made the production better."

Galloway unfolded the list of the cast. "What about Shahan? Has he been with you long?"

Ross pondered the question. "A year or so. He teaches here at Towson High. Been there six or seven years."

"And he never had problems with Sims?"

Ross shook his head emphatically. "Like I said, Mister Galloway, everyone got along well. We never had any serious problems."

Galloway studied Ross a moment, uncertain whether to be impressed or surprised by the man's obvious self-assurance of his cohorts' relationships. "Let's see," Galloway said, glancing at the list. "What about Eric Guidry?"

With a shrug, Ross replied, "Same. No problems. Eric has a landscaping business. His son works with him." He hesitated, then continued. "And the last one is Michael McBride. Young man. Quiet. Works at Wal-Mart in Towson. He's saving his money for a New York fling off Broadway."

Cutting his eyes toward the high school stage, Galloway said, "Does he have the talent?"

With a rueful grin, Ross replied, "It doesn't take a lot of talent. Oh, Mike has it. No question. If he has the staying power, he'll make it."

Galloway studied the slight man. "You've been here how long now?"

"Eleven years." He paused, drew a deep breath, and glanced at his students on the stage. "And they've been worthwhile."

"Where were you before?"

He hesitated momentarily and ran the tip of his tongue over his lips before a tiny grin ticked up one side of his lips. "Where all acting teachers come from, Mister Galloway. New York. Truth is, I had talent, but not enough to take me where I wanted to go. I refused to settle for the small parts. Oh, I tried it for a few years, but—" He shrugged. "We all have egos. I gave in to mine and left the Great White Way, convincing myself the theater would be the poorer for my departure." He chuckled ruefully. "It wasn't."

Galloway nodded, suddenly overcome with the feeling that the director wasn't telling all. "Tell me, Mister Ross. Saturday night. What did you see take place on stage?"

Ross pressed his two middle fingers into his forehead for a few moments, then glanced from Teri back to Galloway. "I've thought about that a lot. Do you believe in happenstance?" He looked from one to the other.

"I suppose so," Teri replied.

"Yeah," said Galloway. "What about it?"

"Well, if George hadn't moved from his spot, the light batten would not have struck him."

Galloway heard Teri catch her breath. He leaned forward,

his pulse speeding up. "Did I hear you right? He wasn't supposed to be at that spot."

"Right." He gave a disbelieving laugh. "I told the sheriff that I would have sworn George stumbled—no, not stumble. Ah . . ." He searched for the right word. "Lurch maybe. It wasn't a smooth step as if you were moving from one spot to the next, and it really wasn't even a lurch. There was just a jerk in the movement that doesn't have a jerk in it." He paused and grinned sheepishly. "And no, I'm not being theatrical, Mister Galloway."

Galloway's brain raced. Lurched? That's exactly what he had seen. He studied the smaller man a moment. "You're certain of that?"

Ross nodded. "Hey. I'm the director. I tell them where to stand. Yeah, I'm certain, as certain as I'm standing here talking to you."

Taking a deep breath, Galloway realized Ross' observation had given birth to a puzzling question. If Sims had lurched from his spot, then where was the deliberation in the murder, the premeditation? He tucked the question back in his growing repository of unanswered puzzles. He replied, "So, how would you account for the—the jerk, the lurch?"

Ross pursed his lipes. "Oh, several ways, I suppose. He could have twisted an ankle, stubbed a toe, even tangled up in his own feet."

"Is that what you think happened?"

"I honestly don't know. I watched the video a dozen times. I saw the jerk, but no sign of his feet getting tangled."

Galloway and Teri exchanged knowing looks, each remembering Galloway's insistence that he had seen something both on the stage and in the video before the tiny flash of light. "Did you see anything else on the video. Other than the cast."

Ross frowned. "Like what?"

"A shadow—I'm not sure—something like a shadow behind Sims."

The thin director gave Galloway a quizzical look. "No. It was night. There were shadows everywhere. All I did see was a flash of light, but that was probably just a reflection from one of the overhead lights on something in the audience."

A profound silence settled over the trio for several moments. Sean Ross had given Galloway that for which he had asked, yet the feeling that Ross had not been completely forthright was overpowering. Well, he reminded himself, there was plenty of time. He nodded to the stage. "What are you working on?"

A broad smile split Ross' slender face. "*Our Town.*"

"One of my favorites," Galloway said.

"Mine too," Ross replied. "Mine too."

Teri looked at Galloway as she snugged down her seatbelt. "He certainly seemed positive about everything."

Galloway glanced at her, amusement in his eyes. "Too positive, too definite."

"I wonder why?"

"I suppose I could play the cynic and say he did it because he didn't want to take a chance on shifting the blame."

A frown knit her brows. "I don't understand."

"I might be grasping at straws, but I've come to believe that when someone is so adamant in a situation like this, often it's because they don't want someone to snoop in the wrong places."

"But, couldn't it simply be that he is absolutely certain?"

Galloway gave her a wry grin. "That too."

Teri arched an eyebrow, and remarked, "This detective business ain't the most scientific work around, is it?"

"Now you're learning," Galloway said.

"Well, at least I thought you had something when he said Sims lurched forward."

"Yeah. Me too." He shook his head and started the pickup. "I'm beginning to wonder if my eyes are playing tricks on me. I'm the only one who's seen the shadow on the video."

She laid her hand on his arm. "Personally, I didn't see Sims lurch forward. But two of you did. Let's take another look when we get back."

"You bet we'll take a look," he replied, anxious to see if the video supported the lack of premeditation. He flexed his fingers about the steering wheel as they pulled back onto the main highway heading for Towson. "Someone's hedging.

Morgan claims Mary Calvin threatened Sims. Her husband denies the accusation, and Sean Ross claims the two got along fine. No problems."

"I believe Frank Calvin. He was telling the truth."

Galloway laughed. "Don't let your feminine prejudice affect the evidence now."

She glared at him. "I'm not letting my feelings influence me, but I do think he was telling the truth."

"So do I," Galloway said.

She looked at him in surprise.

"All I'm saying is that we talked to three different people and came up with three different answers."

"So now what?"

"So now, we talk to Mary Calvin."

"And how do we go about—"

"Look!" Galloway interrupted her. "Turning into the warehouse."

Ahead, a rusty pickup disappeared through the gate into the parking lot of Continental Delivery.

"What is it?"

Galloway slowed, anxious to get a better look at the pickup as they passed the entrance to the parking lot. "That pickup. It's the same model that took a shot at us."

Teri looked at it and noticed something else. "Its back bumper is missing."

Chapter Ten

Galloway pulled onto the shoulder of the highway 50 feet beyond the entrance and stopped. Chinese Tallow trees lined the chain-link fence surrounding the warehouse. Through gaps in the tangle of blackberry bushes and wild roses, they watched as two men in jeans, T-shirts, and caps climbed from the rusty pickup and disappeared into the warehouse.

"Is that it? The pickup?" Teri whispered.

"Could be. Bumper's gone. Back fender's messed up. Left tail-light looks new."

"But, what are they doing here at Continental Delivery. Why . . ." The question died in her throat. She looked at Galloway in disbelief. "You think—Morgan . . ."

With a shrug, Galloway said, "Look what he has to gain."

"But Sims' wife is still a partner, isn't she?"

"So far."

A passing vehicle honked at them.

Galloway glanced at his watch. Almost five. He shifted the pickup into gear and pulled onto a dirt road on the south side of the parking lot. "The warehouse should be closing down about now. Let's find us a spot along here where we can watch without calling attention to ourselves. See where our old boys go."

A few minutes later, the parking lot emptied with the exception of the Chevy pickup and the Viper.

Teri whispered, "Looks like they're shutting down for the night."

Before Galloway could reply, a dark green bobtail truck pulled into the warehouse lot, the name Express Unlimited emblazoned across the side in bright yellow. "Now what?" Galloway muttered.

The bobtail backed up to the loading dock as Morgan and the two men from the old pickup emerged from the warehouse.

Morgan glanced to his left as a black sedan pulled into the parking lot, a cloud of dust billowing up behind it.

"Well, well, well," Galloway whispered as the sedan pulled up at the loading dock.

A figure in a dark suit stepped from the sedan and spoke with Morgan. Morgan tossed him a small plastic bag and gestured to the two men pushing dollies into the bobtail. Moments later, one came out of the bobtail shoving a dolly holding three boxes with words stenciled on the side.

"The guy on the ground sure doesn't look like one of the locals around here," Galloway muttered.

"What do you mean?" Teri whispered, puzzled at the activity on the dock.

"If I'm not mistaken," Galloway replied, "we're watching a drug deal go down."

Teri gasped. "You're kidding!"

Galloway nodded.

As they looked on, one dockhand paused with the loaded dolly until the man in the dark suit inspected the package Morgan had given him. Finally, he nodded to Morgan, and the dockhand wheeled the dolly down a ramp and unloaded the three boxes into the trunk of the sedan. At the same time, the figure in the dark suit slid a suitcase on the dock at Morgan's feet.

Moments later, the sedan drove away, and Morgan carried the suitcase inside the warehouse. The two dockhands continued unloading the bobtail, wheeling the stock from the truck into the warehouse. After the last load, they remained in the warehouse for several minutes.

"Look at that," Galloway said as the two dockhands came from the warehouse. One of them was counting a handful of bills. "Well, looks like Buster Collins might be right. He said he thought Morgan was a broker."

"You think Sims found out, and Morgan killed him?"

"Possible." Galloway chewed on his lip. "Of course, Sims might have been in it with Morgan, and his death was nothing more than a crazy accident."

A frown etched wrinkles in Teri's forehead.

"Or," Galloway added, "it was one partner removing the other."

Moments later, Morgan reappeared with the suitcase. He tossed it in his Viper and spewed gravel from the rear tires as he sped away. Galloway fired up the Silverado. "Let's see if we can find out where our friend is going."

Morgan headed into Towson. Just beyond the courthouse, he parked in front of the Towson Restaurant. Galloway pulled into a parking slot on the opposite side of Main Street, easing the tires against the curb.

Morgan remained in the Viper for a few minutes. When he stepped out, he carried a small satchel. Carefully, he locked the Viper, glanced around the parking lot, then went inside.

In less than five minutes, a man in green uniform with a badge on his chest exited the restaurant, the small satchel in his hand.

"Look," Teri exclaimed. "Isn't that the same bag?"

Galloway jerked his head around. "Look away, fast," he said in a harsh voice. "He's coming this way."

Scarcely breathing, they kept their eyes averted from the approaching stranger. "You think he knows we're watching?" Teri whispered.

"I don't know how. Unless he's one of your psychics."

"You never lose a chance to make fun of them, do you?"

"At least, there's no cold air in here."

"You've gone too far now BJ."

Galloway chuckled, keeping his eyes on the sideview mirror, studying the uniformed man. "Mexican," he said, noting the squat build and dark complexion. He spotted a name-tag above the man's shirt pocket, but the distance was too far to discern the letters.

The squat Hispanic angled to his left and climbed into a pickup three parking slots away. Galloway leaned back in relief. "He's backing out. I'll jot down his license."

"You're not going to follow him?"

"Can't take a chance on Morgan spotting us. We'll just stay right here until they both leave."

Teri adjusted the rearview mirror so she could see across the street. "You were right," she said. "Morgan's standing beside his car watching that guy drive away."

Galloway flipped open his cell phone. "Sit back and relax. I'll call Darla at the office. She'll run a make on this license number."

Teri shook her head. "What would you do without her?"

"I don't want to even think about that. She's the best secretary, file clerk, gopher—you name it. I just bring in the money. She keeps everything else in the office going." He laughed and punched in the number. "Maybe she has the information on Mary Calvin's birth certificate."

Within 10 minutes, Galloway's secretary responded with the data from the license plate. "Luiz Tennessee Garcia. That's some name," Galloway said, studying the slip of paper on which he had jotted the information. "Lives here in Towson."

"You think he's with the sheriff's department?"

"I doubt it. Probably some kind of security company associated with Continental Delivery. That would make sense."

"How's that?" Teri asked.

"Look at the deal. Morgan brokers it. Pays off the guys who unload it as well as someone in security to keep his mouth shut." He shifted around in the seat and looked at Teri. "Garcia could be that security. He looks the other way when a shipment comes in."

"Who does he work for, Continental or another company?"

"I'm guessing another company. Still, it makes no difference." Galloway tapped a finger in the palm of his hand. "Either way, he gets paid."

"You think so, huh?"

With a rueful grin, Galloway replied, "I hope so." He grimaced. "Wish Darla had given us something on the birth certificate, but maybe she'll have it later today. Now, let's finish with the cast of the play. Then we'll see what we can learn about our Tennessee Garcia."

Teri opened the folders. "That'll be Eric Guidry, Michael McBride, and Don Shahan."

As the director had said, McBride was saving his money for a fling at New York. And no, he had never noticed any animosity among the cast. "Everyone worked okay together. Eric and I were on the stage with George when it happened." He shook his head. "It seemed like it was all in slow motion. Maybe that was because it was so dark in there."

Galloway glanced at Teri, then turned back to McBride. "You sure it was just you and Eric on stage. Was there anyone around Sims?"

"No." He drew a deep breath and released it. "Positive. Just me and Eric."

"What about the others in the cast? You happen to notice where they were?"

He gave an apologetic smile. "Not really. You see, they never miss a cue, so I guess they were where they always were, by the pin rail waiting for their entrance."

Fiftysomething Eric Guidry echoed McBride's words. When Galloway questioned him as to his reasons for taking part in the play, Guidry glanced over his shoulder and then gave Galloway a shy grin. "Truth is, I kinda like the spotlight. Oh, I'm no actor. Now, Mike is. He's pretty good. Me, I'm just an old codger having fun. Besides, most people who stay at the inn are fairly well off. You'd be surprised how much landscaping business I pick up from my gig as an actor."

Galloway and Teri laughed. Don Shahan was next.

* * *

David Morgan glanced around the spacious living room of his mansion. As usual, he was alone. His wife was attending the East Texas Soroptimist meeting; his daughter was probably hitting the bars outside of Lufkin with some long-haired, coke-snorting musician; and his son, well, Morgan had no idea where that worthless kid was. Find the pot, and you'd find Warner.

He could never understand just how his own family could have turned out to be so dysfunctional. He muttered a curse and reached for the telephone. Impatiently, he patted his foot on the floor as the phone rang. Finally, someone answered.

"Elton? That you?"

"Yeah, Mister Morgan. What's up?"

"Come on in. Got a special load. Don't bring Caleb."

After a moment, Elton said, "I thought we got all the goods this afternoon."

"Do I look stupid? I know Caleb is connected to Garcia. This is something Garcia don't need to know about. Just you and me. Ten minutes."

Elton replaced the receiver and jumped to his feet. "Back later, sis. Got some work to do."

A Kool cigarette dangling from her lips, Elisha Brister scowled at her brother. "You fix my car like you promised? I got to go to work tonight."

"Yeah. Just don't hot rod it."

Her frown deepened. "I'll have your skin if it leaves me stranded alongside the road. You hear? I've got enough trouble with that witch of a bartender."

He laughed. "It won't," he replied, slamming the door.

Don Shahan lived in a secluded cottage north of Towson. He was a slight six-footer with a ready smile and a shy manner. His recollection of that Saturday night was the same as McBride's and Guidry's. "We had no problems. We all got along together real well."

Galloway studied the younger man a moment. "You look familiar. Have we ever met?"

Shahan's faint smile remained on his lips. "I don't remember. I don't think so."

Galloway shook his head. "Oh, well." He chuckled. "Hope that wasn't my first senior moment."

They all laughed.

"So, you teach history, huh?"

"Yes."

"What made you decide to teach history?"

"Teaching history is an ideal profession for an introvert," Shahan told them in a soft, well-modulated voice without hesitation. "I'm comfortable around children, but I've always had a problem around my peers."

"What about the play? You're with your peers there."

"That's one of the reasons I work in Sean's plays, you know—to force myself to deal with adults. I get along well with the cast."

"Any of the cast have arguments, problems?"

Shahan hesitated, stroking his chin with his thumb and forefingers thoughtfully. The gesture rang a second chord of familiarity with Galloway. "No. Not that I can remember. Oh, we disagreed about things from time to time—you know, small stuff."

Galloway waited, but Shahan remained silent. "Such as? I mean, what do you call small stuff?"

"Nothing for anyone to be upset over. Interpretation of dialogue, gestures—little stuff. Like I said, nothing really bothered us."

"In talking to your director, he said you and Mary were backstage at the time. Where was she standing?"

He shrugged. "I can't say. She was behind me. I was in the wings near the pin rail, waiting my cue." He glanced at Teri. "But, I can't believe she was responsible. The rope just slipped. That's all there was to it."

"But both you and Mary were near the pin rail. Right?"

The slender teacher eyed Galloway suspiciously. "Sure. Off and on during the play, all of us were. We all had the opportunity to yank the pin, but none of us did. I walked past it myself not two minutes before the batten fell. Like I said, I was in the wings waiting for my cue."

Galloway had run out of questions for the time being. "Thanks for your time, Mister Shahan."

In the pickup, Teri scooted around in the seat and stared at Galloway. "What do you think about him?"

"I don't know. He's closemouthed." When he saw the frown on Teri's face, he explained, "You think about it, he didn't volunteer much of anything. He answered the questions, but went no further."

"Maybe it was like he said, he's uncomfortable around his peers."

Galloway chuckled. "Maybe."

The pine forest was dark and silent. The headlights punched lonesome holes in the night as Galloway pulled back on the highway for Towson. "Spooky out here," Teri muttered, glancing about at the tall pines lining the highway, and the complete darkness beneath them.

"Perfect spot for an introvert," Galloway remarked.

"He seems like a nice person."

"Yeah, but I know him from somewhere. I just can't place it." He shrugged. "Oh, well. When we get back to the inn, I want to run a check on Garcia and see what Darla found out about Mary Calvin."

A pair of oncoming headlights glared brightly in his eyes. Before Galloway could blink his lights, the headlights turned off the highway, directly into the parking lot of Continental Delivery Company.

"Somebody working late tonight," he muttered, slowing the Silverado.

"It's that old pickup," Teri said as they passed the entrance. "And look, Morgan's there. That's his sports car."

Galloway continued down the highway a quarter of a mile, then quickly turned off his lights, braked lightly, and made a U-turn, heading back to the side road they had parked on earlier in the day. "Let's see what's going on over there," he muttered.

Chapter Eleven

They parked in the shadows of the tall fence so they could peer through the gaps in the Kudzu vines.

A single light illuminated the loading dock and the parked bobtail. Morgan and one of the laborers Galloway had seen earlier worked quickly, dollying small bales from the truck into the warehouse.

As they watched, a dark pickup with overhead lights pulled into the parking lot and slowly drove around the warehouse. From time to time, a spotlight darted along the tall fence. "Security," Galloway whispered.

When the security truck pulled back on the highway, Galloway opened the door and stepped out. "Wait here. Lock the doors. Don't open them for anyone. If someone comes along, take off. If we get separated, I'll meet you along the highway later tonight."

She looked at him in surprise.

Galloway gestured to the warehouse. "I want to take a closer look." Without another word, he closed the door and vanished into the night.

Moments later, Teri spotted a shadow scurrying across the parking lot and disappearing into the shadows cast by the bobtail truck. "Be careful, Galloway," she whispered. "Be very careful."

* * *

Dressed in his stained boxer shorts and undershirt, Tennessee Garcia sat at the kitchen table, eating jalapeno peppers, washing them down with a bottle of Corona Extra, and studying the stack of money on the table before him. He belched and shot a glance toward the bedroom where his wife of 20 years slept. The four children were in the adjoining bedroom, all sleeping in one bed.

Once again, he counted the money. Almost seventy-five thousand. Enough to go back to his father's little village of Cerraivo and retire for life. His greasy black hair fell in his eyes. He swept it back with short, fat fingers and glared at the bedroom door. No, he could not retire to the life of a *propietario rico*, a rich landlord—not with this wife. She was *grasa la mujer vieja,* a fat old woman. Her feet were growing larger, spreading out flat like the duck. He should find himself a lithesome and lovely girl, a *muchacha encantador,* who would make him very happy.

He scratched his protruding belly and belched once again.

Still, he reminded himself, business was good with Morgan, even after hiring his nephew, Manuel, to work security at Continental. Maybe he should be smart and remain. Morgan would do nothing to endanger him with the law, Garcia told himself. He drained the last of his beer and reminded himself that the warehouse owner had more to lose than he— much more.

With a satisfied grunt, he placed the stacks of bills back into the briefcase and fit it into the opening he had fashioned in the wall behind the refrigerator. After replacing the wall panel and shoving the refrigerator back against the wall, he stepped back and studied the kitchen. No one could find the briefcase. Not even his *bruja*, his hag of a wife.

Behind him, the bed in the bedroom squeaked. He spun, then quickly strode across the room, his eyes narrowing in anger. His wife lay facing him, eyes closed, breathing regularly. For several minutes, he stood watching her.

Satisfied all was well, he returned to the kitchen where he fished another pepper from the gallon can and opened another Corona Extra and turned on the TV.

* * *

Galloway crouched against the radiator of the bobtail. Light from the loading dock flooded along each side of the truck. He heard dull thumps from the two men inside the truck.

Morgan spoke up. "Mine's loaded."

"Mine too, Mister Morgan."

"This is the last of them. Let's get them inside."

The wheels of the dollies clattered as they bounced over the rear lift onto the loading dock. Galloway peered around the side of the bobtail in time to see the two men disappear into the warehouse. Without hesitation, he dashed to the loading dock and pulled himself up.

He paused long enough to glance inside the truck, noting the panels removed from the floor where the smuggled goods had been hidden.

Voices jarred him into action. He pressed up against the warehouse door and peered inside. The two men pushed the dollies into an office with opaque glass walls. Galloway slipped into the warehouse and ducked behind a row of pallets on which were stacked large cardboard cartons.

The office door squeaked open.

A voice carried across the warehouse. "Back tomorrow, Mister Morgan. Same as before?"

"Yeah, Elton. We got another shipment. Remember, Caleb don't need to know about this. He'll leak it to Garcia, and that guy is making enough off me."

"Yes, sir, Mister Morgan. Don't you worry none."

"Just you remember, Elton. Do what I say, and I'll take good care of you."

"Yes, sir, Mister Morgan. Yes, sir."

"Now, close up the truck for me. I'll shut down in here."

"You bet."

The outside door rattled down. Galloway didn't move. Then the truck door slammed shut. Galloway still remained motionless. One by one, the lights went out in the warehouse until only one light remained in the office. Footsteps echoed through the deserted warehouse, and the front door slammed shut. Still, he remained behind the crates, waiting an extra 10 minutes after he heard the squeal of tires as the Viper pulled onto the highway and sped away.

Warily, he peered above the pallet of cartons, studying the warehouse for security cameras. He saw none of the telltale blinking red lights. He hurried across the concrete floor to the office door, which he quickly unlocked with a set of picks.

Inside, he found two dozen duct-tape wrapped bundles stacked in the corner of the office. He shook his head in wonder at Morgan's casual storage of the bundles, each of which appeared to be fifteen or so inches square. He poked the blade of his knife in one, then touched his tongue to the blade. Raising an eyebrow in appreciation, he muttered to himself. "Not bad."

At that moment, the front door of the warehouse opened, banging against the wall. Morgan's angry voice echoed through the cavernous building. "I told you not to come at night. Someone could get suspicious."

The strident words galvanized Galloway into action. He hurried to the door and as the footsteps came closer, slipped from the office and disappeared into the shadows of the warehouse. He ducked behind a stack of crates as Morgan and two burly bikers rounded the corner of the office.

Morgan inserted the key in the lock and turned it. He paused, a frown on his face. He tried the door. It did not open. He turned the key the opposite direction, and the door opened. Still hesitant, he glanced around the warehouse and then at the key in his hand. He could have sworn he locked the door when he left. His eyes narrowed. He knew he had locked it.

"Come on, man," growled one of the bikers, "we want our goods."

The words jarred Morgan from his thoughts. "Huh, oh. All right, all right. Come on in." He shoved the door open, and the three men disappeared inside.

Galloway moved quickly, too quickly. He stumbled over a two-wheel dolly, sending it clattering to the floor. He froze.

One of the bikers jerked the office door open. "What was that?" He turned to Morgan and grabbed the front of his shirt. "You trying to play some kind of trick on us?"

Morgan slapped his hand away. "Don't be a fool. Someone's in here. They must have seen the stuff. Find 'em."

Galloway crouched lower between the stacks of crates.

"Watch the doors," Morgan's voice echoed across the warehouse. Footsteps headed in his direction.

Muttering a curse at his own foolish audacity in even entering the warehouse, Galloway looked around for a means of escape. Then he remembered the broken windows just below the roofline. He peered into the shadows near the ceiling.

The hollow click of footsteps grew closer.

Staying in a crouch, Galloway slipped along the dark corridors between the stacks and cut down an intersecting corridor that led to the back wall of the warehouse. He looked up.

Twenty feet over his head he spotted a casement window with a pane missing. Without hesitation, he climbed up the crates of goods stacked next to the wall. Halfway up, he glanced over his shoulder. All he could see below was row upon row of stacked merchandise.

A guttural voice echoed from the far end of the warehouse. "You see him?"

"Not over here." The voice was Morgan's.

A third voice growled from the opposite end of the warehouse. "Stop yapping and keep looking."

Galloway climbed up on the top crate and grimaced. The opening left by the missing pane was too small for him to slip through. He grinned to himself when he saw that the window opened from the bottom and swung out, locked in place by a short handle.

Gently, Galloway tested the handle. It didn't budge. He cast a furtive glance at the shadows filling the cavernous building, then tapped the heel of his hand against the handle.

It still refused to budge. He tapped it again, harder. Still, no movement. Clenching his teeth, he slammed his hand against the handle. With a chilling snap, the handle broke loose from the window and bounced off the crates, clattering to the concrete floor, sounding to Galloway more like a head-on collision between two cars than a mere window handle.

"The back wall. Over there."

"There he is. Up on the stacks."

Galloway moved quickly, shoving the bottom of the window out until there was enough room for him to squirm through headfirst. He held to the windowsill as he drew his legs through, and then dropped feet first, landing in a crouch.

Immediately, he raced for the chain-link fence and scaled it, dropping into the cushion of pine needles on the floor of the surrounding forest.

Without hesitation, he moved several yards back into the forest and crouched behind a tall pine.

Moments later, dark figures with flashlights appeared beyond the fence, shining piercing beams of light up and down the fence as well as into the forest. They searched along the fence, finally stopping within hearing of Galloway.

Morgan growled, "Whoever it was, we won't find him now. He could be ten feet away in that forest, and we couldn't see him.

Galloway remained behind the pine until well after both the bikers and Morgan had driven from the parking lot.

There was no moon, and the interior of the pine forest was complete darkness—so dark that the only way to move through it was by feeling, extending the hand.

Using the backdrop of the partially illumined parking lot, Galloway eased toward the fence where there was enough peripheral light to see where he was going.

He made his way back to the highway and crouched in the vegetation lining the narrow road. He peered up and down the road. Traffic was light. Ten minutes later, a white Silverado approached.

The dash lights had been turned off, darkening the cab of the pickup, but Galloway recognized Teri behind the wheel as the vehicle passed.

He knew what she was doing, patrolling the highway, expecting him to appear anywhere, everywhere. He'd flag her down next time.

Suddenly, he froze as the headlights of an oncoming car reflected on something off the side of the highway near the curve around which she had just disappeared.

Moving as silently as possible, he eased toward the object. Probably just a sign over which vines had grown, he told himself.

Then he heard voices.

He dropped to the ground and waited.

Twice more, the Silverado drove past.

About the time Galloway figured he would probably spend the night lying on pine needles, a voice carried through the stillness of the night. "Whoever it was, he ain't coming this way."

"Let's get out of here," the second voice said. Moments later, two motorcycles roared to life and sped away.

Galloway flagged Teri down on her next pass.

Chapter Twelve

Even before Galloway slammed the door, Teri asked, "What did you find?"

Glancing out the rear window for the motorcycles, he nodded. "Let's go. I'll tell you on the way back to the inn. And watch your speed. We don't need the sheriff asking questions. Not yet at least."

"Don't worry about me. I pulled out when those bozos came outside with the flashlights. I guessed they were after you." She shook her head and chuckled. "You're always getting in some kind of trouble."

He arched an eyebrow. "I know someone else who's going to get in trouble if she doesn't get us out of here."

"Okay, here we go," Teri laughed. "So, were there more drugs?"

"In spades. A shipment of coke. Uncut." Quickly, he related the events of the last two hours.

"What do you think Morgan's up to?"

"Looks to me he's trying to flim-flam someone, namely Tennessee Garcia."

"You mean the guy in the uniform this afternoon? The one who met Morgan?"

"Yeah. Morgan's pulling a double-cross. He's smuggling goods in under Garcia's nose."

She frowned, but kept her eyes on the narrow road winding its way through the swamp. "I don't follow you."

"We saw Morgan get paid for a shipment. Then, he paid Garcia. At least, Garcia was carrying what appeared to be the same satchel Morgan carried into the restaurant."

"Okay. I follow you so far."

"Tonight, Morgan and some guy named Elton removed coke from the truck, this time from a false floor. Morgan told this Elton guy not to let word get back to Garcia."

The lights from an oncoming car illuminated the wry expression of wonder on Teri's face. "So, a crook is crooking another crook."

"I couldn't have said it better myself."

Ahead the lights of Lloydville winked through the twisted ironwood and drooping cypress of the swamp.

"You think Sims was part of it?"

"Could be. We should have a better handle on it all tomorrow. I'll pay Terp a visit. Maybe he'll let me talk to Mary Calvin. Then I'd like to pay Arlene Sims a visit. Afterward, we'll head over to Delta Downs."

"The race track over in Louisiana? But why?"

"Call me crazy, but this whole case is too loosey-goosey. I mean, look at what we have. First, we have three partners and three or more women with whom one or more partners were having affairs with over the last few years." He paused, then continued. "Sims with Jennifer Pelt, Graves—the old boy who was stabbed in the back—he had affairs with Hoffpauir and Purghan."

"And others," Teri put in. "Remember, Hoffpauir couldn't remember all of them."

"Yeah. So, when you toss smuggled coke and whatever else along with this Mexican called Tennessee Garcia into the mix, you have mass confusion. Enough confusion so that it gives me the uncomfortable feeling that Carl Graves' murder five years ago is somehow tied in to all this. And to top it off, Morgan claims Mary Calvin threatened to kill Sims."

"Okay, so what's at Delta Downs?"

"I have a couple of friends who bet the horses. If Graves lost his money on horses, these guys will know."

Teri slowed as the lights of the inn appeared on the top of

the next rise. "I don't know about you, but speaking of horses, I'm so hungry, I could eat one."

At that moment, Galloway's stomach growled. "Me too," he laughed.

The dining room was closed, so Galloway and Teri had to settle for a ham and cheese sandwich at the bar. "Not exactly a steak, but it'll have to do," Galloway said, grinning.

While they waited for the sandwich, Galloway ran his hand along the underside of the bar. He paused. A grin settled over his face. He felt a tiny hole. Just as he suspected.

Before he had a chance to tell Teri of his discovery, Buster Collins entered the bar. He headed directly toward Galloway and slid up on the bar stool next to him. "What's happening?"

Galloway brought him up to date.

Obviously disappointed, Collins said, "I figured you'd have more than that by now."

Galloway studied the paunchy man. "Don't get impatient. We're a lot farther along now than we were two days ago."

Collins frowned. There was a trace of frustration in his voice. "But, you don't have any idea who did it. Maybe you should—"

"Hold on. I told you Sunday that I did things my way. I don't need any advice. I don't really care whether you believe it or not, but I will find out who killed George Sims. If it is your daughter, then so be it. Now, I'll tell you one more time, be patient. Do we understand each other?"

Collins studied Galloway a moment. "They said you were—"

"Pigheaded?" Galloway grinned.

The paunchy man chuckled and shook his head. "Yeah. All right. I won't say a thing."

"Good. Now tell me. What security companies are around here, either local or national?"

Collins pondered the question a moment. "I use Southeast Texas Security some. They're local. The national companies stay around Lukfin and Woodville, then down around Beaumont and Port Arthur." He shrugged. "I've never had any problems with Southeast. They've always done me a good job."

Galloway slid off the barstool. "Their office in Towson?"

"Yeah."

"Thanks," Galloway said. He glanced around at Teri. "Now, as soon as we finish here, I need to make a phone call."

A glass of bourbon in hand, David Morgan sat in his den, staring blankly at the TV. He had wracked his brain in an effort to figure out the identity of the interloper in his warehouse.

His first thought was Tennessee Garcia, but he quickly discounted the notion for no one, not even Elton, knew the shipment was coming on the same truck with the initial shipment.

Garcia's snitch, Caleb, had seen the empty truck. He had no information to pass along to Garcia.

Morgan began ticking off his buyers, but none of them could have known about the shipment.

On the other hand, it could have been a bum trying to find a place to spend the night.

He turned up his glass and drained it. The incident might have been harmless, without any implication. Morgan pondered the events of the night. Should he cut out the extra shipments for the next few weeks? He grimaced. Do that, and he'd be losing 20 big ones a week.

Back in their room, Galloway called his secretary while Teri showered. To his surprise, a sleepy voice answered. He was expecting voice mail. "Darla? Is that you?"

"Huh? Oh, yeah, yeah, Boss. I had the calls forwarded to my place. I figured you'd want to know about Mary Calvin."

Galloway shook his head. That girl was a jewel. "What did you find out?"

"There's no father listed on the birth certificate. It says unknown. But she was born in Decatur."

For a moment, Galloway puzzled the answer, but then reminded himself the omission could very well have been a

hurt and angry mother wanting to completely erase the identity of her child's father. Nothing surprising there.

"Okay, Darla. Now, I have some more names for you."
Quickly, he provided her the names of the cast and the director.

"Got them. Is that all?"

"No. The last one is a guy by the name of Luiz Garcia.
You ran his license yesterday. He lives in Towson. He might
work for Southeast Security." He paused, then added. "And,
Darla, I need the information fast."

"Don't worry, Boss. I'll run it right now."

He replaced the receiver and sat staring at it, lost in his
own thoughts. A light thumping overhead jarred him from his
contemplations. Suddenly, a tendril of cold air curled around
his neck and just as quickly, disappeared.

An unbidden shiver ran up his back, and an unwanted
thought leaped into his mind. At that moment, the shrill jangle
of the telephone broke the silence. "Who could that be?" he
muttered, picking up the receiver. "Hello."

A deep, jovial voice echoed over the line. "Galloway?"

"Terp? Is that you?"

"Naturally. Heard you were around. Don't you ever visit
old friends anymore?"

"I just learned that you were the sheriff around here," Galloway replied, stretching the truth a tad. "I planned on stopping by tomorrow morning."

"Come on by. I'll show you around."

For the next few minutes, they exchanged pleasantries and
reminisced over old times. Terp finally came to the point.
"Hear you been asking questions, old buddy."

"Some. I didn't want to go any farther without talking to
you." It was a white lie, but a necessary one to pacify the
law.

"Somebody here hire you?"

"Buster Collins."

"Old Buster. Nice guy. He afraid the Sims woman will sue
him?"

"No. Truth is, Terp, Collins doesn't believe Mary Calvin killed George Sims."

"Oh?" His tone was guarded. "Go on."

"He claims Calvin is his daughter, but she doesn't know it. And he doesn't want her to find out." Quickly, Galloway outlined the history of Collins and his family.

Terp whistled. "Look, Galloway. You and me worked just fine together over in Houston. You were always honest and straight with me. Personally, I don't mind you asking around, but I expect you to turn over everything you find to me."

"Like always?"

"Like always?"

Teri paused in the door to the bathroom, her dressing gown snugged around her waist and a puzzled frown wrinkling her forehead. Galloway winked at her as he spoke into the receiver. "You know me, Terp. Whatever you say, I'll do. And I promise not to compromise anything."

"Sounds fair. You run across anything yet?"

"Not really. I wanted to talk to Sims' widow and Mary Calvin tomorrow. You think I can get in to see her?"

"Tell you what. Come on in tomorrow afternoon. You show me what you have so far, and I'll get you in to see Calvin."

"Thanks. See you then." He replaced the receiver and winked at Teri.

"Everything all right?" she asked, sitting on the bed beside him.

He leaned forward and touched his lips to her. "Couldn't be better."

"That's good to know—Beverly." She returned his kiss, deeper, stronger.

Abruptly, the telephone rang.

Irritated, Galloway grabbed it, ready to give Terp Howard a few strong words. "Yeah."

The irritation on his face gave way to surprise. He stared at Teri in disbelief. "Yeah. Yeah, she's right here." He handed Teri the receiver.

Her eyes grew wide as she listened to the voice on the

other end of the line. "Thank the Lord no one was hurt. No. No. I'm coming back." She looked at Galloway who nodded agreement. "I'll be there in a couple of hours. Meet you at the office." Still staring at Galloway in shock, she replaced the receiver. "I can't believe it. One of my shops burned to the ground."

Galloway slid his arm around her shoulders and hugged her to him. "Which one?"

"Number three. The one on Old Spanish Road." She shook her head. "At least no one was hurt, and I have insurance." She forced a feeble smile. "Sorry to put you to all this trouble."

He hugged her again. "No trouble. Get dressed. Let's hit the road."

In the darkness of the attic above the bedroom, Jennifer Pelt sat back on the floor and stared thoughtfully at the tiny beam of light emitting from the small hole through which she had peered as Galloway and Terp Howard spoke on the telephone.

She considered the two pieces of information she had garnered eavesdropping. First, Buster Collins had hired a detective to look into the murder, and second—she shook her head in disbelief. Second, Mary Calvin was Buster's daughter.

Leaning forward, she massaged the ache in her twisted leg. She had laughed when she heard Mary Calvin had been accused of murdering George.

She thought back over the past few years. Unbidden images of her sister came flooding back, bringing to life the pain of her sister's suicide. Jennifer fought the tears filling her eyes. Such a waste. But at least, it was all settled now, had been for five years. Thanks to George, she reminded herself.

A tiny smile played over her lips. Men were so stupid. Her smile grew wider as she remembered her on-again, off-again affair with George Sims. Like Carl Graves, George had a roving eye. Maybe it was the trucking business, but she couldn't complain. He always came back to her. He wasn't much of a lover, but he had provided her with the details of her sister's suicide, and he was generous. Her only complaint was that he died before carrying out his promise of $100,000 if she would leave the state.

Moments later, the beam of light from the hole in the ceiling vanished, followed by the closing of a door from below.

Jennifer remained motionless except for switching on her tiny flashlight. Slowly, she rose to her feet, and shining the beam into the darkness around her, pushed the information she had learned aside. She had more important work before her.

Chapter Thirteen

After dropping Teri off at her apartment, Galloway swung by his place and grabbed some gear, his laptop among the items, and left instructions for his secretary, Darla, to contact him via e-mail.

It was early morning before Galloway drove back into the parking lot at Mystery Inn. He grabbed a short nap, showered, shaved, downed a cup of black coffee, and headed for Towson, anxious to talk to Arlene Sims.

The dark circles under her eyes and her gray-streaked hair in desperate need of a good brushing were mute testimony as to the recent anguish Arlene Sims had endured, but the wan smile when she invited Galloway inside was genuine. "Please excuse the house," she said, leading the way into the kitchen. "The last few days . . ."

"I understand, Mrs. Sims. And I regret having to disturb you, but—"

"Don't apologize. Terp said you would be by." She gestured to a stool at the snack bar. She poured two cups of coffee and slid one before Galloway. "I'll do whatever I can to clear all this up," she added, sliding onto a stool across the snack bar from Galloway. She lit a cigarette. "George never liked for me to smoke in the house. Now, I don't suppose it will hurt." She took a deep drag and blew a stream of smoke toward the ceiling. She coughed once, then said, "Before you ask, I'll tell you right out. Yes, George was unfaithful. I know he had his mistresses, but he provided well for me and the kids. Sent them through college. The boy is a teacher, and the girl is an engineer." She paused and sipped her coffee.

Galloway hesitated, taken aback by her candor. Then he smiled. "Must've been tough."

She shrugged, her hazel eyes reflecting the weariness she felt. "Things are tough for everybody, Mister Galloway. You just make do and don't complain."

He sipped his coffee. "Admirable philosophy, but one I imagine hard to follow."

"You have no idea. Now, what can I do for you?"

He studied his coffee a moment, then looked into her eyes. "I met your husband Saturday before the play. He wanted to hire me. He said he was afraid something would happen to him. He seemed to believe that whoever was after him had something to do with his partner."

"David? David Morgan?"

"No. Carl Graves."

"Carl?" Brows knit, she stared at him in disbelief. Her cigarette dangled from her lips.

"I met your husband outside the room where Graves was murdered. He told me Graves had been his partner. He also said that he believed someone was going to try to kill him like they had Graves."

She shook her head. "I don't understand. That was five years ago. What could one have to do with the other?"

"That's exactly what I'm trying to find out, Mrs. Sims."

For a moment, she studied him, squinting against the smoke drifting up from her cigarette. "All right. Go ahead."

"Did you notice your husband being unusually upset or nervous in the days before he . . . before Saturday?"

"The last few years, George was always uptight, nervous." She took a drag from her cigarette. "Something was always going on," she added, blowing out a stream of smoke. "I never questioned him about his business, but something, I don't know what, but something happened last Wednesday or Thursday. Something put him on edge."

"You didn't ask why?"

Through half-lidded eyes, she studied him with amusement. "I didn't really care, Mister Galloway. As long as he brought in the money to take care of us, I didn't care."

"I take it he didn't talk about it."

She shook her head.

"I heard Graves was a big spender. He gambled and built up some large debts, then borrowed money from the company to pay off his debts."

A glitter like flint flashed in her eyes. "Borrowed? Not quite, Mister Galloway. Embezzled is a better word."

He hid his surprise at her announcement. "Oh?"

She studied him a moment further, then tapped her cigarette in the ashtray. "Carl was a likeable soul. He had one girlfriend after another. And yes, he gambled. Loved it. George and David Morgan tried to hold him down, but they couldn't control him. They tried to buy him out, but he wouldn't sell. Then George and David discovered Carl had been siphoning money from the company to take care of his debts." She paused and chewed on her bottom lip. "What I'm going to tell you could get David in trouble. I don't want that."

Galloway nodded and ran his fingers through his short-cut hair. "I won't hurt anyone who did not take part in your husband's death, Mrs. Sims."

Satisfied, she continued. "Carl had been embezzling from the company for two or three years when George and David discovered it. Carl promised to repay the company if they wouldn't prosecute. Being through all they had together, naturally they agreed. Carl started repaying the money. But, a slow turn in business plus the working capital Carl had stolen put the company on rocky ground." She paused to sip her coffee. She shook her head slowly, her eyes crinkled with amusement. "What the boys didn't know was that Carl was getting his money to pay them back from selling coke and pills. Small time, George said."

She paused to inhale deeply from her cigarette. "Of course, they told him to stop dealing, but they didn't turn him in." She smiled wanly. "They couldn't. Maybe if they had, he wouldn't have been murdered. But they didn't. They couldn't afford to."

Galloway leaned forward. "Why not?"

"Because," she replied, fixing him with a look of defiance, "they decided to sell coke themselves."

"What?" Galloway stared at her, unsure if she were serious or just joking.

"That's right. Carl was small time. They went big time and dealt it themselves until they had the company back on solid footing. Then they did stop. Carl too."

Studying the cup of coffee on the snack bar before him, Galloway framed another question. "Do you think Morgan might have gone back to dealing?"

Arlene Sims touched her tongue to her lips. "Today, in this world, anything is possible, Mister Galloway. Sure, David Morgan might have gone back to dealing. And my George was many things, some I don't even like to think about, but he hated drugs. Now, don't ask me to justify his dealing because I can't. But I honestly think if David had gone back to dealing, and George knew, he would have told me. Except for his women, he was honest with me, which is more than I could have said for Carl Graves. He used women like dirty rags. One, according to George, even killed herself after Carl dumped her." She shook her head. "Really, he was a piece of trash, but he was still a likeable piece of trash." She looked up at Galloway. "Sound crazy?"

"Not at all," he said, smiling warmly at her. "Not at all."

She puffed on her cigarette and her eyes glazed over as she stared through Galloway, peering back into her memories. In a monotone, she said, "I've wondered who killed George. To be truthful, I don't believe it was Mary Calvin. The only time her name ever came up between us was when she worked for Continental. And this was just in passing. You know, when he told me what his day was like." She shrugged. "I don't know. Maybe something happened between them, but I find it very hard to believe."

"Did you ever hear George talk about a man by the name of Garcia? Might have called him Tennessee."

"Tennessee Garcia?" She shook her head. "No."

He tried another angle. "What about George's stockbroker? I heard George was angry over something the stockbroker did."

"Aaron Lyman?"

Galloway shrugged. "I don't know the name."

With an amused gleam in her eyes, she said, "That's him, Aaron Lyman. And yes, that infuriated George. Aaron used some of George's stock as collateral for some of his own deals. George went after Aaron with blood in his eyes. Said he was going to prosecute." She hesitated and giggled. "Sorry. I shouldn't laugh, but looking back it was funny. At the time, it wasn't, but now . . . You see, even though Aaron was guilty as sin, George jumped him so hard that Aaron finally stirred. Now, Aaron is gay, and he threatened to spread the rumor that George was gay, that the two of them were lovers if George didn't back off." She chuckled. "George was stunned. If there is any business that detests gays, it's the trucking industry—them and construction workers. George calmed down in a hurry, long enough for Aaron to apologize and promise full restitution."

"I imagine George found himself another broker."

"In a heartbeat. But Aaron did pay him back."

"You think he could have killed George?"

She shook her head and tapped out her cigarette. "No reason."

Galloway nodded and slipped off the stool. "Thanks for your time, Mrs. Sims. Now, I have one last request. I'd like your permission to look through anything of your husband's if I think it will help us find his killer."

She frowned. "I don't understand."

"It'll simply make any evidence I find legal."

Slowly she nodded. "Fine."

"And if I think of something else, I'd like to come back."

She reached for another cigarette. "You know, George was always fussing at me about my cigarettes. Somehow," she mumbled, glancing around the kitchen, ". . . somehow, smoking isn't as much fun now as it used to be."

* * *

Galloway had almost three hours before his appointment with Terp. He decided to pay Aaron Lyman a visit.

Lyman was the branch manager of the brokerage in Towson. A slender, effeminate man, he eyed Galloway suspiciously after the detective introduced himself and told him the purpose of the visit.

"It was just a broker-client relationship," Lyman explained. "That's all. I don't know what I can tell you."

"That isn't what I heard," Galloway said. "My source said you two were an item."

Lyman's eyes widened in surprise, then he broke into peals of laughter. When he finally caught his breath, he shook his head. "George Sims? Sorry, Mister Galloway. I don't know where you get your information, but it stinks. George was so straight, he'd put an arrow to shame."

"But didn't you once threaten George with that rumor?"

The laughter froze on Lyman's slender face. "How'd you know about that?"

"I told you, I have sources."

He glanced about the gallery of the brokerage, then nodded to a glassed-in office. "Over here."

Inside, Lyman came quickly to the point. "If you know about that rumor threat, then you know what was behind it."

"Yes."

"I paid all the money back. George was satisfied."

"That's what you say." Galloway looked around the brokerage. "If I was a stockbroker, the last thing I'd want is for word to get out that I used a client's stock as collateral for a personal debt. In fact," Galloway laughed, "I might even be tempted to shut someone's mouth, permanently."

Lyman's eyes grew wide. "I didn't have a thing to do with George's death. We haven't spoken since the, ah, since the incident."

"I don't think you had anything to do with it either," Galloway replied abruptly.

The stockbroker frowned. "Then—"

"But, I'm not the sheriff. He might take an entirely different view of the situation." With a casual shrug, he added, "It could make for some juicy talk around town. But I don't want that. All I want is a few honest answers."

Lyman suddenly understood. "I have a good job here. I make good money, and I help others make money. The last thing I want to do is destroy all of this."

Galloway grinned. "Then we understand each other. So tell me, did Sims ever talk to you about his company being in trouble, about needing cash?"

Lyman hesitated. "About eight or nine years ago, George wanted some cash, which didn't surprise me for I had heard one of his partners had some shady dealings with some Mexican."

"Go on."

"According to George, his old man, who was pretty well fixed, refused to part with a cent. So he came to me about borrowing against some of his stocks. That's pretty desperate. A guy has to be in deep trouble to borrow against his portfolio. I figured it was for the company, but before we finalized the paper work, he backed out, saying the woman had been killed in an accident. Truth is, I don't think he realized he had never mentioned the woman to me, but I didn't let on." He chuckled. "His old man died recently, after George didn't need the money."

"How much was his father worth?"

"Couple of million. George was the executor of the will."

"What about brothers and sisters?"

"One of each. Both worthless. The brother, Sydney, is a fiftysomething party animal. The sister, Ola Mae Wilkerson, has lost count of her divorces. I think she's on husband number five now." Lyman paused. A shrewd gleam glittered in his eyes and he leaned forward. "That woman was behind the door when God handed out brains—she's so dumb. A friend of mine is her attorney. The other night, he told us about a call he received from her just after her old man died. She was drunk, but she wanted him to put her in touch with a hitman. She wouldn't say who she wanted wasted, but she wanted someone who could do the job."

"Was it for her brother? George Sims?"

"Seems logical to me. But, I don't know for sure. The nutty woman might have been talking about both brothers."

"So, what did your friend tell her?"

"Drop dead." Lyman laughed.

"What did she say?"

"She cussed him out and slammed the phone down."

"And this—this attorney friend told you all this, huh?"

"Yeah."

"Sounds like a breach of client-attorney privilege to me."

The laughter faded from Lyman's face. "Look, Galloway. This was just a group of us, ah, fellas having a party and telling war stories. You can't say you haven't done the same thing."

Galloway didn't reply. He glanced around the office. "Nice place you have here. I suppose if I need to visit with you again, there won't be a problem."

"No."

Galloway reached for the door. "Good."

"Galloway? About George. What are you going to say about the incident?"

Facing the smaller man, Galloway replied, "Nothing. Unless I find you lied to me."

An expression of relief played over Lyman's face. "I told you the truth."

Chapter Fourteen

Towson County sheriff's office was a red brick, two-story structure on one corner of the courthouse square. Two patrol cars were parked in front. Galloway pulled up beside one and climbed out.

Terp Howard opened the jail door and stood grinning at Galloway.

"You haven't changed much in the eight years since you left Houston—just uglier," Galloway said, laughing as the two friends shook hands.

"You always were jealous," the sheriff growled, slapping Galloway on the shoulder. "Come on inside. Let me show you around the place. The grand tour, so to speak. It ain't much, but I call it home."

"You still not married, huh?"

"Can't find anyone who can tolerate me," the broad-shouldered sheriff said.

"I heard you had a lady friend," Galloway replied, remembering the remark of the clerk at the convenience store.

He shook his head. "Off and on. None that'll tolerate me. Come on. Like I said, there isn't much here, so the tour will be short."

The tour took five minutes. Three quarters of the first floor were the sheriff's office. The remainder was his living quarters.

"Voters expect you to stay right on the job, huh?"

Terp flashed a grin. "Sure do. Upstairs is the cell block."

Galloway peered up the narrow flight of stairs. "That where Mary Calvin is?"

The grin faded from Terp's square face. "I don't cotton to having women in my jail. It just don't seem right, but . . ." He shrugged his shoulders.

Galloway chuckled. "Still a softy, huh?"

Terp cut his eyes toward the grinning Galloway. He smiled when he saw the laughter in his old friend's eyes. "Yeah. That's why I couldn't make it in Houston. You had to be hard-tailed. Wasn't worth it to me."

"How many do you have on your staff here?"

"Staff?" Terp laughed. "That's one of those city words, son. You're in the country now." He nodded to a slender deputy bent over a desk. "Hey, Brock."

The young man looked around.

"Meet half of my staff, Deputy Ernest Brocklin. Brock. Meet Galloway, a big city PI." The young deputy rose and nodded.

Terp continued. "The other half of my staff is out on patrol. John Collins. Good man. Both of them."

"The sheriff tells everyone that," Deputy Brocklin said, grinning broadly. "Helps him keep his job. You out here on vacation?"

Terp glanced at Galloway, then nodded to the deputy. "Brock, go take a run around town. Me and Galloway need to talk."

The young deputy shifted his gaze to Terp. "Yes, sir, Boss."

When the door closed behind Brock, Terp gestured to his desk. "Have a seat." He plopped down in the chair behind the desk. "Okay, bring me up to date."

Leaving nothing out, Galloway summarized the last few days, including the attempts on his life as well as the drug deal he had witnessed at the warehouse. "Even with all that, Terp, I don't really have a handle on things. There are too many loose ends. Nothing really ties together. Still, I can't help believing that somehow, Sims' death is connected with Carl Graves' five years ago. The stockbroker, Aaron Lyman, mentioned that Graves got into some shady dealings with a Mexican."

Terp leaned forward. "He say Graves by name?"

"No. But, Graves was the only partner to get into big financial trouble back then. Sims and Morgan bailed him out. That's probably where Morgan met Garcia." He paused, sorting his thoughts. "Now, I know Morgan and Garcia are working together. Like I told you, I heard Morgan tell one of his men, a guy by the name of Elton—"

"That would be Elton Brister. His family lives back out in the woods. Regular East Texas Pineywoods rednecks. He's got a sister working out where you're staying."

Galloway hesitated. "Her name wouldn't be Elisha, would it?"

Terp arched an eyebrow. "Yeah. How'd you know?"

"Just a guess. Anyway, Morgan told Elton to keep quiet. He didn't want Garcia to know about the delivery."

Leaning back in his chair and steepling his fingers on his chest, Terp said, "Sounds like Sims might have stumbled on to something."

"If he did, he didn't tell his wife. I asked her."

The sheriff arched an eyebrow. Skepticism edged his words. "She really believes he would have told her?"

Galloway nodded. "According to her, he was honest with her on everything except his women. I think she's right."

Terp raised an eyebrow. "Hard to believe. Maybe he didn't have time to tell her."

"I don't know. She said something had been bothering him for a couple days prior to Saturday. Maybe he just hadn't gotten around to telling her."

Taking a deep breath, Terp leaned forward. "So, where do you stand now? What's next?"

"I plan on interviewing Sims' brother and sister. She sounds nutty as the proverbial fruitcake, but she was trying to find a hitman. Word is Sims was executor of their old man's estate. If she needed money, and he was out of the picture, she might be the one to take over. I've seen crazier things."

Terp shook his head in disgust. "Sounds just like Ola Mae.

Ola Mae Wilkerson. Drinks like a fish, spends like there's no tomorrow, and a couple of peas short of a casserole. Tries to run with the society crowd, but she can't stay sober long enough to make it to first base."

With a shrug, Galloway replied, "Sounds like a winner. I hope she'll be sober enough to talk to me."

"Try to get there before sunrise," Terp said with a chuckle.

Galloway nodded. "So, now you know everything I've done. It's my turn. Tell me about Mary Calvin."

"Not much to tell." The sheriff shrugged his wide shoulders. "According to Morgan and Elton Brister, she threatened to kill Sims. She'd gone out to the warehouse to take her husband his lunch. Her and Sims got into some kind of argument. Morgan and Elton drove up. When they were climbing out of the pickup, they heard her scream at Sims that she would kill him if he fired her husband, and then she slapped the whey out of him."

"What did she say about that?"

"Nothing, except she didn't kill him. Oh, she admitted she threatened him, but that's all it was, a threat. But still," he added, "we have motive; we have opportunity; we have the weapon. Cut and dried, Galloway. As cut and dried as anything we faced back in Houston."

Galloway remembered his earlier interview with Morgan on Monday morning. At the time, Morgan thought the death was an accident. Now, he turns out to be one of the accusers. "You say Morgan and this Elton Brister are the ones who claimed she threatened Sims?"

"Yeah. Elton came to us early Sunday morning. Said he'd heard about Sims and figured we should know about the threat. Morgan was out of town. Shreveport if I remember right. He verified it when I talked to him Sunday afternoon."

Galloway arched an eyebrow. So, Morgan had been out of town as he said. "Have you talked to the director of the play, Sean Ross?"

"Some. Why?"

"Did he tell you Sims missed his mark that night; that he stumbled under the falling batten."

"I don't understand."

"If Sims had stayed where he was supposed to on the stage, the batten wouldn't have hit him. He stumbled and fell under the stage lights. Makes me wonder if someone had been just trying to scare him."

Terp shook his head. "He didn't tell me all of that. He said Sims stumbled. But even so, someone pulled the pin releasing the rope. It might have been Mary Calvin just wanting to frighten Sims, but she killed him. It might not be murder, but it's manslaughter." He hesitated, then leaned forward and reached for the radio. He called Deputy Brocklin. "Go talk to Sean Ross at school. Get the details from him about Sims stumbling under the batten Saturday night."

He looked at Galloway. "We'll turn it over to the DA, okay?"

Galloway nodded. "Now, what do you know about the members of the cast? Ross seemed antsy when I was talking to him."

With a shrug, Terp replied, "Not much more than others around. He and his wife came here from New York. I don't think she's too crazy about the backwoods out here. They've had a couple of problems. Nothing serious, just the typical beauty shop gossip of a small town."

"How about the teacher? Shahan."

Terp grimaced. "Good teacher. Good man. Does a lot of volunteer work." He hesitated.

"But?"

"Well, I don't know. It's just rumors, talk—probably nothing more than malicious rumors."

"Go on."

Terp leaned forward. "First, I want you to understand he has given me no reason at all to believe the rumors, but because he is so soft-spoken and laidback, word went around that he was gay. He hangs out with Aaron Lyman at times, and I know Aaron's sexual preference. But, I don't know about Shahan for sure. If he isn't, then he's mighty dumb. You remember the old saying, if you're going to sleep with dogs, don't complain about the fleas."

Suddenly Galloway remembered where he had seen Don Shahan. The Purple Sleeve Nightclub, one of the classier gay bars in Houston. He kept the information to himself, but made a mental note to contact Aaron Lyman again. "What about the others?"

"The others, McBride and Guidry, they're just what they seem. McBride grew up here. What I hear is that he's saving up to head to New York. Guidry is just an old country boy who likes to act."

Galloway considered the information Terp had provided. "Okay. Now can I see Mary Calvin?"

Mary Calvin looked up from where she sat on her bunk reading. She smiled weakly at Terp. "Hello, Sheriff." The smile fled her slender face when she saw Galloway.

Terp spoke gently. "Don't be alarmed, Mary. This is BJ Galloway. He's here to try to help you."

A frown replaced the alarm on her pale face. She rose and stepped to the door. "I—I have a lawyer," she said to Galloway.

"I'm no lawyer, Mary. I'm a private investigator. I've been hired to prove your innocence."

The frown deepened. She smoothed her short, brown hair. "Hired? Who hired you? We don't have the money for a detective."

"That isn't important. What is important is that I want to find out just what really happened that night."

She glanced up at Terp for reassurance. "He's telling you the truth, Mary. I've known Galloway for fifteen years. He's an honest man. You can trust him."

For a moment, she hesitated, then stepped back. "If you say so, Sheriff."

Terp gestured to Galloway. "Go on in."

Galloway pointed to the lock. "Unlock it."

"Huh?" The sheriff knit his brows. "Oh. Sorry. I forgot. It isn't locked," he said, swinging the door open. When he saw the confused look on Galloway's face, he explained, "Mary's the only one here. No sense in locking her up. This way she needs to stretch her legs or something, she can." He indicated the bathroom at the end of the hall.

Galloway stepped inside. "Only in Texas," he muttered.

Terp headed downstairs. "I'll leave you two alone. Just come on back down when you finish, Galloway."

Mary stood staring up at Galloway like a recalcitrant child. He smiled. "Want to sit?"

"If you do."

"I wouldn't mind. My feet are killing me." He sat on one cot, and Mary demurely sat on the edge of hers. She laid the book in her hand beside her on the cot. It was the Bible.

"You have a beautiful family," he said. "I met them yesterday."

Her eyes shone. "I'm very lucky. Frank and I have been blessed."

At that moment, Galloway found himself hoping that Mary Calvin was innocent. "Tell me what you know about Saturday night."

She closed her eyes and pressed the fingers of one hand against her lips, a posture she held for several seconds. Finally, she drew a deep breath and opened her eyes. "It's hard for me to think about. I feel guilty in a way because a part of me is relieved that George is dead, but the other part cries because a child of God has been taken from the world."

Galloway remained silent, waiting.

Mary folded her hands in her lap and fixed her eyes on his. Her voice trembled with emotion. "I can only tell you what I saw. I was backstage, waiting for my cue. Sean and Don were with me. I was watching Eric—he is Artis, the gambler in the play. When Eric took a step toward George—that was my cue to enter. He, ah, he . . ." Her breathing speeded up. She hesitated and clenched her bottom lip between her teeth for several seconds until she regained her composure. "Just before Eric started toward George, the light batten fell. Another three seconds, and I would have been on stage." She paused and released a long breath of air. "That was all I saw."

"But, you say Don Shahan and Sean Ross were with you in the wings."

"Yes."

"Can you remember where they were standing?"

She thought for a moment. "Sean is usually by the pin rail. Don was . . ." She shook her head. "I'm sorry. I can't remember, but he was there. We were talking. I just don't remember exactly where he was standing. Is it—is it terribly important?"

"Just asking, Mary. Nothing to upset yourself about. Now, the threat you made on Sims. What was it all about?"

She shrugged her slight shoulders and dropped her gaze to her hands folded in her lap. "I already told the sheriff."

"I know, but tell me."

With a weary sigh, she glanced up and then lowered her gaze once again. "There isn't much to tell. Frank had forgotten his lunch that day. I made his favorite sandwiches, chipped beef. I took them and some hot French fries to him, and George followed me back outside. He said he was going to fire Frank, and I told him I'd kill him if he did. That's it."

Galloway frowned. Something was missing in her story. "Why was he going to fire Frank?"

In a tentative voice, she replied, "George . . . George was like that. He liked to throw his weight around."

"Maybe so, Mary. But he had to have a reason. Was Frank goofing off or something?"

Her eyes blazed. "Don't even think such a thing. Frank is the hardest, most conscientious worker that Continental Delivery has. He would never goof off."

"Then there's more, Mary. There has to be. What is it you haven't told me?" He leaned forward and laid his hand on hers. "All I want to do is help, but you've got to let me help you. Why did George Sims threaten to fire Frank?"

She looked up, tears filling her eyes. She shook her head slowly. "I can't tell you. I can't tell anyone."

"You have to, Mary. Not just for your sake, but for Frank's. And for your children."

For several long moments, she stared at Galloway, tears rolling down her cheeks as she struggled with whether or not to reveal the secret she carried in her heart.

Gently, Galloway whispered, "It will be just between you and me, Mary. I promise." He had no idea how he would keep the promise, but he would.

Slowly, she nodded. "Years ago, George Sims and I were lovers."

Chapter Fifteen

A sudden chill settled over the stark jail cell. Mary shivered, and continued her story. "Before Frank ever came to work at Continental, I was George's secretary. Each of the partners had his own secretary. I was pretty wild back then. Fresh out of high school, a year of business school. My mother had passed away. I never knew my father. I was all on my own, and I wanted to have fun. Ours was just a fling for a few months, and then George found someone else. I didn't mind for by then I had met Frank." She paused, and a soft light filled her eyes. "It was love at first sight." She glanced up at Galloway. "I never told Frank about George, and during all those years since, George was always proper. We were in some plays together out at the inn. He was always the gentleman. Never made any advances until about two months ago."

"Outside the warehouse?"

She looked at him in surprise. "How—how did you know?"

He smiled. "I did my homework. What happened then?"

"Well, George saw me from the office when I gave Frank his lunch. He followed me outside and suggested we take a weekend trip to New Orleans. I thought he was joking at first, but insisted. Then he threatened to fire Frank if I didn't go with him. When I refused, he said he was going to tell Frank about us."

"And that's when you made the threat."

"Yes." She nodded slowly, and a gleam of satisfaction glittered in her eyes. "And I slapped the dickens out of him."

Galloway laughed. "I'm glad."

A faint smile played over her lips. "It felt good."

Though Galloway wanted to believe in Mary Calvin's innocence, he realized the evidence pointed at her. She had a dandy motive, she was present, and she had access to the weapon. More than one poor soul ended up at Huntsville State Prison on less evidence.

What Galloway had to do was dig up evidence left by the real killer. Unlike juries, lawyers, and courts, evidence never lied. It remained where it occurred, waiting to be discovered, analyzed, and interpreted.

"From all I've learned, George Sims was a promiscuous man."

She nodded, remaining silent.

"After you left the company, what did you hear about him and his, ah—"

"Girls?" She smiled. "I'm no Pollyanna, Mister Galloway. Yes, George had them. Carl Graves had them. Even David Morgan. All the partners. I don't remember the names of all the women. I was happy with Frank. And George, to his credit, was good at keeping his affairs quiet. Otherwise, he appeared to be the model husband and father."

A tiny thought began nagging at Galloway. "You remember when Carl Graves was murdered?"

"Yes. Why?"

"You remember any talk, any gossip about who might have been involved?"

She pondered the question a moment. "Just rumors."

"Such as?"

"Well, there was some talk about a drug deal gone bad. Word around was that Carl owed some big money and turned to dealing to pay it off." She shook her head. "But that was just talk."

"Think there was anything to it?"

"I don't like to think so. Carl was always nice to me. Oh, he flirted and all that, but he was just a fun-loving guy. Like

I said, he had his share of women just like George and David. But for the most part, it was all kept quiet. The only time there was any talk was sometime after Frank and I married, some woman died in a car accident on the road north of Towson. There was some gossip she'd been carrying on with one of them, but I never heard any more about it."

"Did you ever have occasion to meet or see a Mexican guy by the name of Garcia?"

"Tennessee? Sure. He was always seeing Carl. Polite and quiet."

"What did they have to do with each other?"

She shook her head. "I can't say. Probably Carl's secretary could tell you. Joyce Purghan was his secretary about then. I left ten years ago. She came in about a year before I left. She might know."

Sitting at the desk downstairs, Galloway related his interview with Mary Calvin, leaving out, as he had promised, her affair with Sims.

"Too bad someone didn't hear Sims proposition her," Terp said.

"I wouldn't mind talking to this Elton Brister. If they heard part of the conversation, they should have heard the rest."

"Be my guest, but right now, I want to talk about the drug exchange you saw."

Galloway winced, fearful Terp might take immediate action. "You know what I told you. From what I could tell, this is an ongoing operation. They have no reason to suspect anything. Give me a few days before you start coming down on the operation."

An expression of uncertainty wrinkled the sheriff's forehead. "From the way you described it, Galloway, it's bringing in some big bucks."

"No doubt. It's an ideal setup. But, all I need are a few days."

"I don't want to lose these guys."

"You won't. Morgan is a fixture in Towson. So is Garcia. Putting together what I've learned, I think Garcia and Carl

Graves worked together; then after Graves' death, Garcia and Morgan hooked up. Maybe Sims stayed in. I don't know." He paused. "But, look at it this way. If Morgan and Garcia have been dealing for the last five years, there's no way they plan on leaving unless they get wind that we're onto them. And they won't as long as it stays between you and me. That's why a few days can't hurt."

Terp studied Galloway for several seconds. "All right. Three days."

"Three? Come on, Terp."

The sheriff shook his head. "Look, if something happens, and the town finds out I knew about it and did nothing, I'm out of a job. Besides," he added, breaking out into a grin, "a big city detective like you can solve a little old hick crime like this in no time."

Galloway shook his head. "You're full of it, Terp. Did you know that? Full of it. I just hope you're not too full of it to remember the woman who was killed in a car wreck out north of town eight or nine years ago."

He considered the question. "That was around the time I took office. Maybe a little before. I don't remember it, but I can find the details for you if it's important."

Galloway shrugged. "I don't know if it is or not, but I'd appreciate it."

Galloway wasted no time when he left the jail. He headed northeast for Lufkin and Joyce Purghan.

The afternoon was a typical autumn afternoon in east Texas. The vast forests stretched in every direction, tall pines blocking the afternoon sun and casting early evening shadows across the highway.

The closer he drew to Lufkin, the heavier the traffic, commuters leaving their city jobs for homes in the stillness of the great pine forests. From time to time, he glimpsed pastoral scenes of rolling meadows of lush grass fenced in by mute columns of towering loblolly pines, luxuriant pastures dotted with glassy ponds reflecting the clear blue sky above. Animals grazed contentedly.

Near a small stream, he spotted three deer gazing upon the passing traffic with casual indifference.

David Morgan looked up at the knock on the door. He recognized the silhouette of Elton Brister through the opaque glass. He pursed his lips, wondering what Elton had on his mind. One of the reasons Morgan kept the young man around was that the rawboned country boy knew his place and, if necessary, he could turn mean. He never presumed friendship with Morgan. In fact, Morgan had quickly realized that Elton preferred the boss-employee status. So, whatever he had on his mind today, it wasn't chitchat or shooting the breeze. "Come on in, Elton."

The door opened, and Elton looked in sheepishly. "Sorry to bother you, Mister Morgan, but I heard something I figured you might want to know about."

Morgan nodded for him to continue.

"Well, sir. There's this detective nosing around about Mister Sims' death. He's been asking a lot of questions about a lot of people."

"You talking about the one that was out here Monday?"

"Yeah. Now, I ain't too bright, but I got to wondering in maybe that was him out here Monday night. I wondered if maybe if it was, then maybe he seen us unloading the truck."

Morgan had himself wondered about Galloway, but he had summarily dismissed the idea. He could see no reason for the detective to be snooping around the warehouse at night. On the other hand, how was Elton aware of the intruder? Morgan had spoken of the incident to no one. That meant one of the bikers had run off at the mouth. Casually, he asked, "Who'd you hear this from, Elton?"

The lanky man shuffled his feet and scratched the weeklong growth of black whiskers on his face. He had to be careful how he answered for he didn't want to give away the fact that he had helped Caleb carry out a couple jobs Garcia had ordered. He was still Morgan's man, but that didn't mean he couldn't earn a few extra dollars from the Mexican even if Morgan didn't like him. "Well, Mister Morgan, it was from Caleb."

"Caleb? How'd he hear about it?"

"Down at Towson Bar. Shooting pool. He said some of them good old boys over there was talking about it." Elton grinned to himself. There was no way Morgan could pin down that explanation.

Morgan eyed Elton shrewdly. "What else did Caleb have to say?"

With a shrug, Elton said, "Not much. Just that some folks are getting worried." He winced as the words left his lips. That was too much. Morgan would know exactly who he meant, but he relaxed when Morgan failed to react to the last remark.

Pushing back from his desk, Morgan rose and stretched. "Well, Elton. Let's just don't worry about it. All this big city detective is doing is trying to find a loophole for Mary Calvin. He doesn't care about us."

Backing away, Elton nodded. "I just—I just figured you needed to know."

"And I appreciate it. Now, close the door on the way out, you hear. Go ahead and clock out. Drink an extra beer for me."

Elton laughed. "Yes, sir, Mister Morgan. I sure will."

After the door closed, Morgan's face twisted in anger. Elton's words, *some folks are getting worried* echoed in his ears. He knew who that someone was. Tennessee Garcia. If that fool pulled some dumb stunt to spoil the operation, Morgan promised himself he would personally get rid of that greasy Mexican.

Galloway braked to a halt when he turned the corner on Meadowgreen, the street on which Joyce Purghan lived. Halfway down the block, three police cruisers and an ambulance were parked in front of a neat brick house. A cold chill ran up Galloway's spine.

He pulled to the curb and joined the growing crowd around the house. "What's going on," he asked a teenager who was gawking at the scene.

"Somebody is hurt or dead, I think. That's what I heard."

"Who lives there?"

He shrugged. "Middle-aged old woman by name of Purghan. I think Ma said her first name was Joyce."

A sense of frustration washed over Galloway. He cursed himself for not trying to interview her sooner. Still, whoever was hurt didn't necessarily have to be Joyce Purghan.

But it was.

Word raced through the crowd. "Joyce Purghan is dead."

Chapter Sixteen

Galloway considered his quandary. He had three days to learn the truth. Three days to unravel the Gordian Knot. Maybe he would be better off to follow the example of Alexander the Great and slice the knot in two. The only problem was knowing where to slice.

On the surface, the solution appeared simple. There was no argument that only three individuals were backstage when the batten fell; Mary Calvin, Sean Ross, and Don Shahan. Mary was preparing her entrance. Sean was to her right at the pin rail. She couldn't remember where Shahan stood.

Sean Ross' recollection of their positions in the wings differed with that of Mary Calvin, and Don Shahan's agreed with neither, although the history teacher's frequenting of gay bars had considerably diminished his credibility as far as Galloway was concerned.

As he pulled onto the highway for the drive back to Towson, Galloway tried to convince himself that one of only three individuals could have pulled the pin, but each time he replayed the evidence, something nagged at him. Whatever it was, it proved as elusive as the nebulous ghosts back at Mystery Inn.

Still the only one of the three with motive was Mary Calvin. Unless . . . suppose Sims' sister had succeeded in hiring someone to take care of her brother. Was there any reason it might not have been Sean Ross, the director, or Don Shahan, the actor? Money had been known to transcend morality.

A sign alongside the highway caught his attention. It pointed east to Vinton, Louisiana, home of the Delta Downs Racetrack. On impulse, Galloway made the turnoff, deciding to take a chance on running down Charley Boudreaux at the track.

The horses weren't running, but the slots were. Galloway paused just inside the door, then headed for the bar beneath the mezzanine. He spotted Charley Boudreaux perched on a barstool with his racing sheet spread out before him on the bar, his snap brimmed hat shoved to the back of his head, revealing a growing expanse of shiny forehead. He sipped bourbon neat.

Galloway stopped behind the older man. "Winning any money?"

Charley glanced around. "Huh? Who?" His eyes lit when he recognized Galloway. He spun himself around and clasped Galloway's hand eagerly. "Well, I'll be—what the Sam Hill you doing over in these part of the woods? You lost?"

Laughing, Galloway shook his old friend's hand. "Nope. I came looking especially for you." He backed off a step and surveyed the older man. "You don't look like you've aged much. That bourbon must be doing a good job of preserving your ugly old hide."

Charley chuckled. "Clean living. That's what does it. No wine, women, or song." He gestured to the next stool and then to the bartender for two bourbons.

Galloway slid up on the stool. "That'll be the day. You always did have one or two good-lookers tagging after you. I can't imagine you've changed that much."

"No. Don't suppose I have," Charley replied, his eyes twinkling. "What brings you over here? The horses? I got a few sure things coming up tonight."

Galloway sipped the bourbon. "Information, Charley. About a man who played the horses here five or six years back."

Charley frowned, his face wrinkling like a French accordion. "Lord, Galloway. I can't remember five days back, much less five years. What's going on?"

Ignoring the older man's question, Galloway continued. "The guy's name is Carl Graves. He died five years back. Word is that he played the horses and at one time owed a bundle of cash over here."

Charley Boudreaux's eyes grew wide, and a grin played over his weathered face. "Carl Graves? Now, that's a name just about everybody over here remembers." He shook his head and chuckled. "That old boy owed everyone at one time or another. I never seen anyone like him."

Galloway shoved his bourbon aside and leaned forward. "Tell me about him, Charley. Whatever you can remember."

The old man shook his head. "I don't know where to start. He played the horses. He won big, and he lost big."

"He ever get in too deep with any bookies?"

With a cackle, Charley nodded. "All the time. But, sooner or later, he got things paid off." He paused and studied Galloway. "What's this all about?"

"I don't know for sure," Galloway replied, shaking his head. "I don't even know what I'm looking for, Charley. I'm just hoping I'll recognize it when I hear it or see it. Did he owe enough for someone to waste him?"

Charley Boudreaux considered the question several seconds, then shook his head. "No. Not over here. Oh, some put the squeeze on him, but like I said, he always came through."

Galloway studied his tumbler of bourbon. "I heard he was quite the ladies man."

"I suppose, but he never let that interfere with his gambling." He chuckled. "That man loved to gamble. Nothing could slow him down."

"What about when the woman he was dating got killed? That slow him down any?"

Charley stared at Galloway, puzzled. He shook his head. "I never heard nothing like that."

Now, it was Galloway's turn to be puzzled. Arlene Sims had told him one of the women Carl had dated had been killed. Mary Calvin was uncertain which of the two partners the woman had dated. Or had he misunderstood? "You don't remember any talk about some woman in a car wreck?"

Charley nodded. "Yeah. But not Graves' woman. He told us about it. One of his partners. I don't remember the name, but one of his partners dumped some woman who went out, and ran her car into a tree."

A surge of excitement raced through Galloway's veins. "Which partner?"

The older man thought for a moment, then shook his head. "Sorry. Don't remember."

Holding his breath, Galloway said, "Think, Charley. George Sims or David Morgan?"

Charley's forehead wrinkled in thought. He shook his head in frustration. "Naw. I'm sorry, Galloway. I just don't remember."

Terp Howard tossed a folder on the desk. "Here's what you asked about. The accident out north of town."

Galloway reached for the folder.

The sheriff continued. "Carol Ann Moses. Twenty-nine. Came from Lufkin. Worked in Towson at Wal-Mart. Three months pregnant."

Shaking his head, Galloway muttered, "What a shame." He skimmed a copy of the death certificate. "Accidental, huh? Just ran off the road?" He looked up at Terp.

"That's what it says," he said wryly. "But, look at the accident report. No sign of the brakes being engaged at all. It ain't no accident when someone deliberately runs their car into a tree."

"What?"

Terp nodded. "This happened just before I was elected. I'd heard about it more or less, but since it was settled before my time, I didn't pay any attention." He gave a rueful chuckle. "The entire resolution of the case smacks of country politics, old friend. Her old man was a bigwing in Lufkin and county politics. Doesn't look good that his daughter killed herself, especially since she was three months with child."

Galloway studied the accident report for several more seconds. With a grim smile, he tossed the folder back on the desk. "Same politics we have back in Houston."

"You been by to see Ola Mae yet?"

Galloway remembered Terp's recommendation. "Not yet. I figure on going over there in the morning." He held up two fingers. "Two questions. First, who was old man Sims' attorney, and second, where is your local paper?"

"I don't know about the lawyer. The newspaper is two blocks over on the right, *The Daily News*. Judd Hampton is the owner and editor." He glanced at his watch. "It's late. Let me call and see if he's still there." Moments later, he replaced the receiver. "You're lucky. Judd's working late tonight. He can tell you who old man Sims' lawyer was."

Galloway winked at Terp. "Thanks, buddy."

Galloway was interested in Carol Ann Moses, enough so he wanted to learn more about her family. In the archives of *The Daily News*, he found her obituary. Father, Samuel J. Moses; mother, Margaret; sister, Jennifer Moses Pelt.

The last name hit him between the eyes. Jennifer Pelt. It had to be one and the same. How many women shared such an unusual surname?

Before he left the news office, the editor provided him with the name of Sims' attorney.

During the drive back to the inn, Galloway considered the two women, Ola Mae Wilkerson and Jennifer Pelt.

Ola Mae had motive. She needed money, and with the death of her older brother, she could become executrix of the will. According to the stockbroker, Aaron Lyman, that could have meant an extra few hundred thousand dollars. The only way she could have managed the hit would have been with help from one of the three in the wings. He nodded. The theory had some possibilities.

And then there was Jennifer Pelt, for whom he drew up one theory after another. What if Carol Ann had been having an affair with George Sims? He could have dumped her when she turned up pregnant. It was a dandy motive. Revenge. Jennifer Pelt could have killed George Sims in revenge for her sister's death.

On the other hand, she wasn't at the play. She was in the bar with Sarah Hoffpauir and then they both went home. Besides, how did she get onstage to release the batten? And if she did, how could she have been deliberately planning to murder him when he actually stumbled into the batten? Could it be she was just trying to scare him? Was she clever enough for those kind of mind games?

Try as he could, Galloway couldn't place her at the scene convincingly enough to satisfy his own suspicions. Yet, she was the sister of Carol Ann Moses, who committed suicide by driving her car into a pine.

To had to his confusion, he was caught between two opposing accusations; one from Arlene Sims, who asserted Carol Ann Moses dated Carl Graves; one from Charley Boudreaux, who didn't know with whom she had an affair, except it wasn't with Carl Graves; and the third from Mary Calvin who knew only that it was one of the two partners. But then Aaron Lyman stated that George had told him he didn't need to borrow against his stock because the woman had killed herself. Was this the same woman?

Galloway leaned toward Arlene Sims' assertions. He couldn't convince himself that Pelt would have had an affair with the man who impregnated her sister and then drove her to suicide.

Back at the inn, Galloway unpacked his laptop, set up his satellite connectivity unit, and picked up his e-mail.

Chapter Seventeen

Galloway shook his head as he stared at the e-mail his secretary had sent him. Using a combination of sources from public records, civil records, family court records, and probate courts, Darla provided Galloway with solid motives for two additional suspects, Sean Ross, whose wife had an affair with George Sims, and Don Shahan, who had met Sims at the Purple Sleeve Nightclub in Houston. But there was nothing on Luiz Tennessee Garcia.

He poured himself a bourbon and reread the information. He had learned long ago that the secret to investigative work was thorough research, which included asking questions— questions about any and everything. Sooner or later, a crack would appear in the shell of the egg, and usually, without warning, the shell split and the information poured out.

When he walked into the sheriff's office earlier, he had only one suspect with a motive. He left the office with two, adding Ola Mae Wilkerson. Thirty minutes later, he added a third, Jennifer Pelt. And now, with the information his secretary had provided, he added two more, Sean Ross and Don Shahan.

He checked his watch. It was late, too late for any further questioning. On impulse, he called Terp Howard.

A sleepy sheriff answered. Galloway blurted out, "I need a favor. Sims' probate attorney is Lum Green. Find out who the executor of the old man's will is now that George is dead. I figure it is Ola Mae, but I want to be sure."

Terp read the implication in Galloway's request. "You serious? You think Ola Mae did have something to do with it?"

"It's a possibility. From what I learned, she and her husband are so far in debt, they'll never get out. I also heard her father was well off. Maybe she figured if she became executrix, she could pick up an extra few hundred thousand. You've seen it just like me. Folks have killed for a lot less."

"You have any proof?"

Galloway hesitated. "No. Just a hunch. I'm seeing her first thing in the morning."

At 4 A.M., the phone awakened Galloway. It was Terp. "Your hunch was right. Ola Mae is the executrix."

Galloway went right back to sleep, content now that the investigation was going his way.

Galloway rose before the sun. He had a full day ahead of him. A few other early risers were in the dining room when he arrived. As he sipped his coffee and toyed with his pancakes, he couldn't help overhearing three guests at the next table whispering excitedly about the noises they overheard the night before.

"I tell you," one said, "it was the ghost."

"I felt the cold air going up the stairs," another put in. "Didn't you?"

The third guest spoke in a tone of disappointment. "No, but I heard the thumping in the attic. I thought it was just a rat."

"Oh, no," said the first guest. "It was that guy who got killed last Saturday. What was his name?"

"You mean George Sims?"

"Yeah. That one."

Galloway downed the last of his coffee. He shook his head. He'd figured out the cold air at the bar, but not the stairs, nor the noises. Was there something to them? He chided himself. Don't be ridiculous. A sudden pain struck him in the back, just below his left shoulder.

"I tell you, there are ghosts in this place," concluded the first guest.

His first stop was Ola Mae Sims Wilkerson. He waited across the street until her husband had left before he knocked on the door.

When Ola Mae opened the door, Galloway understood why Terp had suggested he interview her early in the day. With a cocktail in one hand and cigarette in the other, she eyed him like a cat studying its prey. She invited Galloway inside after he introduced himself and assured her Sheriff Terp Howard knew he was here.

He followed her into the kitchen, noting the worn chenille bathrobe drawn tightly about her thick waist and frizzled hair that had obviously not seen a comb that morning.

If he expected any denials from her, he was surprised.

"Yeah. I know I'm in charge of the will now, and I intend to do what I can to keep that million from going to some cancer research fund."

They were sitting at the kitchen table, wrought iron and glass, obviously expensive. She leaned back and took a deep drag on her cigarette. "None of us agreed with Father, but George was too timid to buck him even after he was dead."

"Maybe George just wanted to honor his father's last request," Galloway offered, keeping his voice level to hide the growing dislike for Ola Mae Wilkerson.

She snorted. "Like I said, George was a wimp. Oh, I loved him. He was my brother, but . . ." She shook her head. "In this world, you got to take what you want. I wanted my share of that million."

"Enough to put your brother out of the way?"

She met his eyes, her own filled with defiance. "Enough to consider it, Mister Galloway. I'm a lot of things, but hypocrite isn't one. Yeah, I even looked into it, but I couldn't do it. He was blood kin. Decent folks don't do that."

Galloway suppressed a rueful smile. "Where were you Saturday night?"

She held up her glass. With an expression of weariness on

her face, she replied, "Where I am every Saturday night. Here in my house getting plastered."

He nodded. "You know a Don Shahan or Sean Ross?"

"Sure. They both teach at the high school."

"They ever have any problems with your brother?"

"Some. Not Don, but Ross and George had words once. George's eyes wandered, and Ross' wife wandered." She chuckled. "Like two wanderers in the night except they didn't pass each other."

Galloway remembered the information Darla had supplied him. It verified Ola Mae's remark. "What happened?"

Ola Mae drained her drink. "Nothing. George found another love interest. Ross and his wife had problems for a while, but they straightened them out. I guess they did; they're still together."

"Don't you have another brother?"

"Sydney. A couple years younger. He's just a younger version of George," she answered, a sneer in her tone.

"So actually, you benefited from George's death."

She eyed him squarely. "If you mean because I'm not going to let that million go to charity, yeah. Syd too. Arlene too. She's George's wife—I mean, widow. Pretty good luck, huh?"

Galloway disliked Ola Mae Wilkerson, but he couldn't help admiring her candor. "I'd say very good luck."

She pushed herself to her feet and opened a cabinet door from which she pulled a bottle of vodka. "I know I had motive, Mister Galloway. And you're probably toying with the idea I paid someone to pull it off. I don't blame you." She looked up from building her drink. "But I didn't kill my brother."

Galloway studied the outside of the Wilkerson house before he drove away. For some strange reason, he believed Ola Mae, yet not so firmly that he would not follow through on his theories. Ola Mae had motive, and she also had enough audacity to explain in one breath how she toyed with the idea of killing her brother and in the next, deny any complicity.

She could have hired Ross or Shahan. Or, he reminded himself, she could have hired Mary Calvin. The latter was highly unlikely, but Galloway wasn't going to overlook any angle.

Ross was his next stop.

The diminutive director was in his office behind the high school stage. When he saw Galloway, a smile leaped to his lips at the same time a frown wrinkled his forehead. "Mister Galloway. Come in. Have a seat. How's the investigation going?"

"Can't complain, but I have a couple more questions, Mister Ross. I'm sure you can clarify them."

Ross' smile faded ever so slightly. "I'll try, Mister Galloway. What do you need to know?"

"I heard that you and George Sims had words some time back involving your wife."

Ross' smile vanished. His eyes grew hard. Galloway spotted the bulging vein on the side of the small man's neck. Slowly Ross nodded. "That was three or four years ago, Mister Galloway. It was just a small problem. The first time my wife and I ever had any problems. I'd forgotten all about it."

"Oh? Then I guess you forgot that you filed for divorce in New Jersey eleven years ago. Sounds like more than a small problem."

Ross gaped at him. "How—I mean—"

"I have sources. So don't tell me the incident just slipped your mind, Mister Ross. No one ever forgets when a spouse breaks the marriage vows."

He shook his head emphatically. "We've got it all straightened out. That was long ago. A man can forget."

"Maybe so. As I remember, you told me the cast got along well. Just minor problems. Sims and your wife doesn't sound minor to me."

Ross eyes turned to flint. "I didn't know you were talking personal problems also, Mister Galloway. You asked about the cast. I just assumed you meant problems relating to the cast and its productions."

Galloway knew the smaller man was lying. Ross had deliberately left out any reference to the incident because he knew it would add up to a motive—a blasted good motive.

"Well, Mister Ross. I'll take the blame for not being more specific. Now, what was the situation all about?"

The smaller man made an effort to relax. He stared down at the desktop. "I don't mind telling you about it. It was a painful time in my life—in our lives. I learned about the affair after their second date. I confronted Sims. He was twice my size, but I was furious." He paused and looked up, a twinkle in his eyes. "It was nothing to laugh about at the time, but what was so funny was that George didn't even argue. He wasn't belligerent, defensive—he was none of the things an adulterer should be. It was like a game of marbles to him. All he said was, 'Sorry, Sean. It won't happen again.' " Ross shook his head. "What really made me angry was later when I stopped to think about it, he demonstrated an absolute lack of feeling or compassion for my wife. To him, she was just another marble in his game."

For several moments, Galloway studied Sean Ross.

Finally, unnerved by the silence, Ross said, "That's the truth, Mister Galloway."

"I believe you, Ross, but I'll let you in on what the sheriff is going to think. You admitted Sims was a terrible actor. I think you even said he couldn't play straight man to the Three Stooges. Well you see, Mister Ross, the sheriff's going to figure you kept Sims in the cast over the years until everyone had forgotten about the incident. Then when you thought it was safe, you made your play."

Ross opened his mouth to protest, but Galloway held up his hand. "You don't have to convince me. Like I said, I believe you, but you might as well be ready for a few visits from the sheriff."

During the drive to Don Shahan's, Galloway considered the different angles from which he could approach Shahan. Darla had provided information, which, though sketchy, could have some substance.

The sun was directly overhead when Galloway pulled up in front of the cabin. As he climbed out, he noticed a man in the backyard wearing overalls with a net over his head. He was bent over a beehive, smoke pouring from the spout of the canister in his hand.

Galloway made his way out back, taking care to stay some distance from the beehives. The man looked up. When he spotted Galloway, he waved and called out, "Another five minutes. I'm almost finished here."

Shahan pulled out a rectangular frame bulging with honeycomb. Gently, he scraped the bees from the honeycomb back into the hive, and placed the frame in a tub that contained several more full frames. He then replaced the frame with one containing simply a sheet of wax, which provided the bees material for them to build their combs.

After fitting the top back on the hive, he carried the tub of full frames toward the cabin, and toward Galloway. A few bees still buzzed around the tub. Shahan laughed when he spotted Galloway backing away.

"They won't bother you, Mister Galloway. They're only interested in the honey. Come on inside." He led the way into a rear room with several machines. "This is where I harvest and bottle the honey," he said, setting the tub on the floor and removing his hat and net. He gestured to a door. "How about a beer. That was hot work. It's cool in the kitchen."

He handed Galloway a long-neck Budweiser. "All I got."

"Good enough," Galloway replied, twisting off the cap.

Shahan turned his bottle up and took several large gulps. He sighed and shook his head. "That hits the spot. Now, Mister Galloway, to what do I owe the pleasure of your visit?"

Galloway leaned back in his chair. Just before he sipped the beer, he said, "Tell me about the Purple Sleeve Nightclub."

Shahan's face blanched. "W-what?"

"You know," Galloway replied casually, "the Purple Sleeve. The private club in south Houston."

Shahan opened his lips but no words came out. His hands shook. "I—I—"

"Maybe this will help," Galloway said, unfolding a sheet

of paper from his shirt pocket and laying it in front of Shahan. "It's your arrest record when the Purple Sleeve was raided."

Shahan swallowed hard. With a trembling hand, he picked up the document.

"Don't misunderstand, Shahan," Galloway remarked indifferently. "I'm not really concerned about the Purple Sleeve being a gay bar. What's interesting are some of the others who were arrested with you—George Sims and Carol Ann Moses to be exact."

Chapter Eighteen

His face pale, his breath coming in short gasps, Don Shahan sat motionless, staring blankly at the sheet of paper in his hand. After a few more moments, his breathing slowed. He closed his eyes and leaned back, resignation all over his face. He shook his head, his eyes remaining closed. "I should have known that sooner or later, someone would find out." He opened his eyes and stared at Galloway. With a shrug of his shoulders, he added, "Okay. So you know. Now what?"

Galloway took another sip of beer. "So, tell me about it."

Shahan slid his beer aside and pushed back from the table. "I need something stronger." He reached into the cabinet and retrieved a liter of Jim Beam, black label. While he poured a stiff drink, he said, "I don't know why we were busted that night. The police knew about the place. It was a private club. They usually didn't mess with us. But they did that night." He sipped his bourbon and slid back in his chair. "George wasn't a regular. He was straight, but from time to time, he'd show up with a lady friend who was curious as to what life was like on the other side."

"What do you mean, he wasn't a regular?"

Shahan shrugged. "Once every two months. You know, in town for the night—show the little lady something exotic to warm things up."

"And he had Moses with him that night?"

Shahan ran his fingers through his blond hair. "Yeah."

131

"How many times were they there?"

"I don't remember. Not too many though. I never paid him much attention. Once, just before the bust, one of his partners came with him. He had a date."

"Which partner was that?"

"The one who got killed a few years back, Carl Graves."

"Who was his date?"

Shahan shook his head slowly. "I didn't know. Never saw her again, but the other one, the Moses woman, she came back by herself, several times."

"How'd you learn her name if you only knew Sims by sight?"

"Once, she asked me for the names of some of the ladies who frequented our club."

Galloway remembered how adamantly Arlene Sims insisted Carol Ann Moses dated Carl Graves. On the other hand, Aaron Lyman believed she was the one for whom George Sims had been attempting to raise money. "Did she ever come in with Carl Graves, the other partner?"

Don Shahan chewed on his bottom lip, then slowly shook his head. "If she did, I never saw them."

"But you did see her several times afterward."

"Yeah, by herself—looking for action." Shahan indicated the copy of the arrest record. "How'd you get that? They didn't press any charges down at the station. We were out of there within a few hours."

Galloway chuckled. "That's one of the quirks of the law, Shahan. Even if no charges are filed, a copy of your arrest remains on record—forever. Unless you expunge it," he added. "Okay, so George Sims showed up there from time to time. How did you get to know each other?"

"I knew his name, but he only knew me by sight."

"So how'd you end up over here?"

He gulped down the remainder of his bourbon. "I knew he had a business over here, and I was ready to make a major change in my life. I'd sown enough wild oats. My roommate contracted AIDS. The doctor doesn't know exactly why, but something in my system holds off the virus." He paused to pour another drink. "Truth is, I figured God was giving me one last chance. I didn't want to screw it up, so I talked George into helping me get a teaching job over here."

Galloway arched an eyebrow.

"Okay, so George wasn't crazy about helping me. He was afraid someone would find out. The rumor mill in small towns like Towson can devastate a career."

"Why did he help you then?"

Shahan hesitated, studying Galloway warily. Finally, he gave a wry grin. "Why not? My life here is probably shot to pieces. He helped me, Mister Galloway, because I threatened to tell the community he visited the gay bars." With a shrug, he added, "That simple."

Galloway tried unsuccessfully to suppress a grin of his own. "At least, you're honest.'

"And to answer your next question, no, the kids, the parents, no one over here knows about me. Moreover, Mister Galloway, they're in no danger from me. I've been straight now for several years, even before I came over here."

For several moments, Galloway studied the condensation beading on his bottle of beer. He believed Shahan, but his motive was compelling. "You know, you have one heck of a motive. George Sims could have threatened to expose you, so you killed him."

The teacher reached for the bottle of bourbon. He paused before pouring. "That's true, Mister Galloway, but he didn't. In fact, he wouldn't expose me because he was more afraid of being discovered than I was."

Galloway studied Shahan filling his glass with bourbon. He had a point, a good point. "You know Aaron Lyman?"

"Yeah, why?"

"You want to keep your secret around here, stay away from him."

Shahan studied Galloway for several seconds. "Thanks. I will."

As the Silverado pickup approached the city limits, Galloway decided that Carol Ann Moses had her affair with George Sims, and not Carl Graves as Arlene Sims had insisted.

As he passed the city limits, he took a right, heading for Jennifer Pelt's. But, if the affair was between Moses and Sims, what on God's earth could possess Jennifer Pelt to have her own affair with the man, who, in all probability, was responsible for her sister's pregnancy and subsequent death?

He shook his head as he parked in front of her house. "She couldn't have known," he muttered. "That's the only explanation." But, he told himself, why didn't she know?

And like the proverbial ton of bricks, the answer struck him between the eyes. Jennifer Pelt didn't know because George Sims put the blame on someone else, and who better than the only unmarried partner he had—Carl Graves.

Wearing a lacy white blouse and sheath skirt cinched in at the waist with a black belt, Jennifer Pelt led the way into the living room of the neat bungalow. She walked with a pronounced limp.

Even though Galloway would rank a one on a scale of one to ten as an expert on home decorating, he was impressed with the Early American décor. The brightly patterned drapes and the red-and-white checked ruffles around the bottom of the sofa and chairs gave him the feeling of being in a dollhouse.

She offered him a cushioned rocker while she sat across the coffee table from him on the couch. Using the remote, she lowered the sound of the TV. A petite woman, she had to sit on the edge of the sofa to rest her feet on the floor. She folded her hands in her lap. With a smile that lacked warmth, she said, "The sheriff said you would be by, Mister Galloway. How can I help you?"

Galloway leaned back. He decided not to mention her sister yet. "Just a couple of fast questions, Ms. Pelt. How long had you been acquainted with George Sims?"

Her eyes twinkled. "Come now, Mister Galloway. You probably know that better than me."

He laughed. "Touché. I have talked to quite a few folks. But tell me anyway."

A trace of warmth came into her smile. "Six or seven years,

I guess. Maybe a little longer. And yes, I knew he was married."

"Any ideas about who might have wanted him dead?"

"As you know by now, George played around. I imagine there are a few husbands who don't regret his death, but none I can think of who have the stomach to kill him."

"Sean Ross and Don Shahan. Would either of them have a reason?"

She considered the question a moment, then shook her head. "No. None of the cast. Not even Mary Calvin. She's a nice kid—well, compared to me, she's a kid. She couldn't hurt a fly."

"Did George seem upset about anything in the last few weeks?"

Pelt stared at her folded hands. "Not until last week. About Thursday or so."

"What happened?"

"I don't know for sure. He called Friday. Said he'd call back, that he had to talk to David about a phone call he had received."

"Did he tell you what was said?"

"No." She grew thoughtful. "But, I imagine it's on his recorder."

Galloway blinked. "Recorder?" He held his breath, refusing to believe his good luck until she repeated her words.

"Yes. George didn't trust voice mail. He recorded all his calls. Said the recordings kept him from making mistakes with client orders." She paused and blinked her eyes against the sudden tears. "I never talked to him again."

He suppressed the excitement surging through his veins. "But you were at the inn Saturday night?"

A single tear rolled down her cheek. "Yes. I went to the séance, and we were to meet after the play."

Galloway suppressed a frown. Sarah Hoffpauir had stated that on Saturday she and Pelt had a drink after the séance, then went home. Now, Pelt refuted the alibi. She claimed she remained until after the play. "But you didn't go to the play."

She gave a half-shrug. "I've seen it before. It really isn't very good. I stayed in the bar. That's where I heard about George."

"From what I hear, you're a regular at the séances along with Sarah Hoffpauir."

A light blush tinged her cheeks. "So I imagine you know why I always go when the medium is trying to reach Carl."

"For the money?"

"Yes. I know it sounds foolish, but people like Carl who die violently cannot find peace in the beyond. They try to come back. They hope to find the peace they left behind."

"Was he a good friend of yours?"

Her smile twisted into a sneer. "I detested him. Whoever killed the louse did the world a favor."

Her vehemence surprised Galloway, but no more than the sudden transformation in her personality. Her eyes grew cold, and she set her jaw. She hissed. "He was scum. He was the most despicable, the slimiest—the way he treated women. I felt unclean just being around him."

"Were you around him much?"

"By myself? Only once. And that was enough. The day before Carl died, I delivered a folder of documents to him as a favor to George. Carl was in his apartment working on some books for Wholesale Supplies out of Shreveport." She shivered. "Like I said, I felt dirty around him. Any decent woman would."

"You have remarkable memory."

With a faint frown, she replied, "Why is that?"

"To remember those details after all this time."

Her face grew hard. "Let me tell you about that. After I gave Carl the folder, he leered at me and tapped his finger on the accounting book and said, why didn't I wait around until he finished with Wholesale Supplies and then we could have our own private party. That's how I remember those details, Mister Galloway." She paused and drew a deep breath. She narrowed her eyes. "He deserved what he got."

Galloway nodded, remaining silent while she cooled down. He looked around her bungalow. "Nice little place you have here."

"Thanks. Sorry about the outburst."

"No problem. Tell me, how'd you get along with the other partner, David Morgan?"

"We hated each other." She shook her head. "Don't be offended, but I'll never understand men. They can go out, cheat on their wives, and think nothing about it. But, let a divorced woman date a married man, and they believe she's the tramp of the century." She shook her head. "No offense intended, Mister Galloway, but I've never figured out just what part of the anatomy men think with."

"A familiar observation, Ms. Pelt. No offense taken. Of course, you know that David Morgan holds you in about the same regard."

"Do I look like I care?"

"Not especially."

"That's because I don't. David claimed more than once that I was blackmailing George. I'm surprised he didn't tell you."

"Oh, he did. He claimed you were blackmailing George to the tune of about a hundred thousand."

Jennifer Pelt shook her head. "He has the amount right, but not the explanation." Before Galloway could ask, she continued, "I knew that George and I couldn't last. He would never leave Arlene and the children. After I'd wasted a few years of a life that was quickly passing me by, I decided to make a break. He offered me money, a hundred thousand, if I wanted it." She gave a wry laugh. "I'm not stupid, Mister Galloway. And I don't worry too much about ethics. So I agreed. I put my place here up for sale. Got an offer two weeks ago. Looks like it's going through. Wouldn't you know?"

"Why do you think George's partners and you never got along?"

She leaned forward and laid her hand on her right calf. "Despite my bad leg, I'm an attractive woman, wouldn't you say so, Mister Galloway?"

Momentarily taken aback, he nodded. "Yeah. Certainly."

"I wouldn't date them. And to men like Carl and David, who pride themselves on their ability to seduce women, there has to be something wrong with someone like me. Don't misunderstand. I'm not bragging, but women know these things. Men don't."

Her response amused Galloway. "In other words, either play the game my way or I'll take my ball and bat and go home."

Her smile broadened. "Exactly."

Chapter Nineteen

After leaving Pelt, Galloway's first stop was the local real estate office. He inquired of the availability of Pelt's house, only to be informed it had been purchased a few weeks earlier. "Guy's credit is good. We'll probably close in a couple more weeks," the realtor said. "However, I have another one just like it."

Declining the offer, Galloway headed into town. It was mid-afternoon, and he was hungry. While downing a hamburger and coffee at the Towson Restaurant, he went back over his interview with Jennifer Pelt. The hundred thousand was one story against the other. She could have twisted selling the house to her own advantage. And she claimed she was in the bar during the play while Sarah Hoffpauir, a proclaimed good friend, said they had both left for home. And then there was the telephone call Sims had mentioned to her.

One thing for certain, he told himself. She was very sure of herself. But, somewhere in the back of his head, he sensed a loose end that didn't quite fit into place.

He drained the last of his coffee, left a five on the table to cover the bill plus a tip, then headed back to his pickup. First things first. Sarah Hoffpauir, then Myrt, the bartender.

Wearing a neat, blue uniform, Sarah Hoffpauir frowned when she saw Galloway step up to the counter in the post office. After an uncertain pause, she said, "Mister Galloway. Can I help you?"

He glanced around the empty lobby. "I need to ask you a couple more questions if you can find the time."

She glanced nervously over her shoulder. "I don't know, Mister Galloway. We're pretty short today."

"It'll only take a minute. It's about Jennifer Pelt."

"Jennifer?" She paused and looked around again.

Before she could reply, Galloway said, "Jennifer Pelt says she didn't leave the inn the other night like you said."

Something close to alarm flashed in her eyes. "She what?"

He nodded. "Yeah. Remember? You said the two of you left the bar together and went home. She says she didn't."

Like a frightened animal, Hoffpauir's eyes cut from side to side.

Galloway tried to put her at ease. "No problem, Sarah. I just figured you were confused. After all, a lot happened that night."

"Yeah. You're right. There was a lot going on." She remained silent for several seconds, her frown deepening. Abruptly, she turned and called to a nearby clerk. "Kathy. Watch the counter for me for just a minute, will you, please?" She indicated a door in the middle of the wall containing mailboxes. "I'll meet you over there."

She looked Galloway in the eye as she closed the door behind her. "I should have known better than try to lie, Mister Galloway." She shrugged her shoulders and grimaced. "I thought it would help. Not that I believe Jennifer had anything to do with it, you understand."

He nodded. "Go on."

"We were in the séance together, then I went to the bar and stayed there during the play, but not with Jennifer like I told you. I don't know where she was."

"She said she was in the bar."

Hoffpauir shook her head. "Not with me. I didn't see her. You see, we've known each other for a long time. That's why after you and that nice woman friend of yours left, I called Jennifer and told her what I'd said to you. She thanked me and then told me that she'd left right after the séance because she was feeling ill. But, well, as I was leaving, I would have sworn I saw her car, a white one, parked at the back of the parking lot where all the azaleas grow."

"What kind of car?"

She shrugged helplessly. "All I know about cars is their color."

"No problem. So, you're saying, she might have still been at the inn."

"Yes—well, maybe. I can't swear it was her car, but in the dark it looked like it." She nodded emphatically. "She works there part-time, but she's always out there, even when she isn't working."

"Oh? Why's that?"

"Why, searching for the money, naturally."

Suddenly, another corridor of suspicion opened for Galloway. Pelt worked at the inn. Temporary helpers were practically invisible. She might have slipped backstage and somehow disengaged the pin.

But why? Lover's revenge?

"And that's the truth, Mister Galloway. The honest to goodness truth."

Sarah Hoffpauir's words jarred Galloway from his thoughts. "Huh? Oh, yeah. Thanks."

She smiled apologetically. "I'm sorry if I caused you any problems."

He smiled back. "Not to worry."

Galloway drove past Continental Delivery, trying to decide his best approach to obtain the telephone recording of the conversation Sims had mentioned to Jennifer Pelt.

Morgan's Viper was nowhere to be seen, but several pickups including the old Dodge were parked in the lot.

There was no choice. Back in Houston, he could have utilized any number of disguises. Here, he would have to utilize the night.

* * *

Back at the inn, he checked his e-mail. Nothing. He sent Darla another name, Jennifer Pelt, then skipped dinner for a bourbon, neat.

Myrt slid the bourbon in front of him. "Well, Mister Galloway, still detecting?"

He laughed. "Sometimes I wonder. By the way, you worked last Saturday night, didn't you?"

She snorted. "Yeah. And I was some upset." He frowned, and Myrt continued. "My relief didn't show up, but I gave her a piece of my mind the next morning."

Galloway sipped his drink as she continued. "Can't get dependable help any more. She claimed she didn't know she was supposed to work, but that's a crock. Just like her brother, too, lazy to work."

Half-listening, Galloway replied, "Her brother?"

"Yeah. Jerk named Elton Brister. Her name's Elisha. Works the dining room and the bar, when she feels like working," Myrt added sarcastically.

Galloway gestured to his face. "Always frowning?"

Myrt grinned. "That's her. Talk about a sourpuss. Why, she fusses so much that even old Caleb, dumb as he is, gets mad at her. And when them two get mad at each other, it's like World War II all over again."

"Caleb?" The name struck a familiar chord.

"Yeah. Caleb Worster. Works at Continental Delivery. Him and Elisha been seeing each other as long as anybody can remember."

Then Galloway remembered the night he had watched Morgan and Elton unload the drugs. Caleb was the one Morgan insisted that Elton say nothing to of the drugs. "Last Saturday night, Myrt, was Sarah Hoffpauir, here in the bar during the play?"

Without hesitation, Myrt nodded. "Yeah. She was the one I was complaining to about my relief not showing up."

"What about Jennifer Pelt? Was she here?"

"During the play?"

"Yeah."

"No. I didn't see her—not then."

Galloway leaned forward.

Myrt continued. "I saw her later. She was driving out of the parking lot about two-thirty when I climbed into my car."

"You sure it was her?"

"You bet. I'd recognize that white Pontiac of hers anywhere. I got one just like it except mine is red."

Pursing his lips, Galloway turned a couple questions over in his head. "Was she working that night? I heard she was temporary help here."

"No. Reason I know is because I looked at the schedule when Elisha didn't show up to relieve me. Jennifer wasn't on it for that night."

"But she is out here often?"

"Yeah. A lot. Bubba figures she's looking for the money."

"You think it's here somewhere?"

With a cynical grunt, she said, "No way."

Smoke hung heavy in the Towson Bar. Half-a-dozen bearded lumberjacks and oilfield roughnecks perched on stools around the bar, cigarettes dangling from their lips, thick fingers curled about sweaty cans of beer. Two couples, arms wound around each other, shuffled around on the postage stamp-sized dance floor, bathed in the red and green lights flashing from the jukebox.

His cap set on the back of his head, Elton Brister leaned over the pool table in the rear of the smoky room and lined up a shot. Caleb Worster, thin as the pool cue on which he leaned, looked on.

The jangle of a telephone cut through the undercurrent of rough voices and drunken laughter.

The bartender who was drawing a draft beer shouted, "Caleb. Grab the phone for me."

Keeping his eyes on Elton's shot, Caleb sidestepped to the pay phone on the wall between the two restrooms. He reached for the receiver, but hesitated as Elton struck the cue ball. The cue ball caromed off the red-striped two ball, sending it toward the corner pocket. Caleb used his best body English to make the two ball miss.

It didn't.

Muttering a curse, Caleb yanked the receiver to his ear.

"Yeah? Towson Bar." He listened a moment, then stuck the receiver toward Elton. "Hey, Lucky. It's for you."

With a grin, Brister took the receiver. "Skill, buddy. Skill." He spoke into the receiver. "Yeah. Oh, hi Mister Morgan." He nodded as he listened. His gaze flicked to Caleb, who shook his head as if to say no.

"Yeah, Mister Morgan. Sure. He's here. We're shooting a game of pool." He paused again, then nodded. "Midnight in the warehouse. Yes, sir, we'll be there."

"What did you do that for?" Caleb demanded as Elton returned to the game. "I was supposed to meet Elisha tonight when she got off work."

Elton shook his head in affected disgust. "You and my sister can wait 'til later to make out. We got a load to take care of. It must be a big one because Mister Morgan put the truck inside the warehouse."

Caleb studied his pool partner. Greed filled his eyes. "I wonder what it is."

"Beats me. We'll find out soon enough. Your shot."

Caleb hesitated. He scratched the five-day-old beard on his gaunt cheeks. "Hey. I just had me an idea. Why don't we get there early and see what the goods are in the truck."

"Why would we do something like that?"

"Because, stupid, we might pick up something for ourselves if we get there before Morgan. We can open the truck and tell him we was just getting ready. After the last few years, he'd believe us."

"I don't know," Elton replied. "We got us a good thing going here anyway. I'd sure hate to screw it up."

"Come on. Nobody's got to know except you and me. And if there ain't nothing there, then there ain't. Besides, after all we've done for him, we deserve it."

Elton pondered the suggestion. Finally, he nodded and slid his pool cue on the table. "Okay then, but let's go. I want to get there good and early before Morgan does."

Chapter Twenty

Back in his room, Galloway tried to collect his thoughts. Beginning with Mary Calvin, there were at least seven suspects, all with sound motives.

Mary Calvin didn't want Sims to fire her husband.

Sean Ross' wife had an affair with Sims.

Don Shahan knew Sims through a gay bar.

Ola Mae Wilkerson wanted her share of a million dollars.

Aaron Lyman had used Sims' stocks for his own gain.

Jennifer Pelt, according to Morgan, had blackmailed Sims.

And, Galloway told himself, David Morgan could be a sleeper. He could have wanted the whole drug business for himself.

The only problem with Wilkerson, Lyman, Pelt, and Morgan was the lack of opportunity. And the possibility wasn't so far-fetched that Jennifer Pelt, being a temporary helper, had not slipped backstage.

That left Morgan, Lyman, and Wilkerson, all of whom had money to pay for the hit—but who? And how?

The cracks in the shell of the egg were growing wider, but not wide enough to reveal any substantial evidence.

Galloway glanced at his watch. Nine-thirty. He arose and poured a stiff bourbon and downed it in one gulp. He grabbed a package of Mystery Inn matches from the ashtray on the vanity and dropped them in his pocket in case the office lights were off.

If he left around eleven, he would reach Continental Delivery at eleven-thirty. His only concern was the security guard making his rounds in the pickup.

A creak in the ceiling over his head caught his attention. He glanced up, thinking of Carl Graves and the stories of the inn being haunted. On impulse, he decided to take a look at the room where the man had been murdered.

On the flight of stairs to the third floor, a presence of cold air enveloped Galloway. He paused and knelt on the stair treads. He studied the wallpaper carefully. He discovered an almost invisible hole in the wall. I'm learning all your secrets, Buster, he told himself with a grin as he rose and continued to the third floor.

Galloway opened the door to the murder room and turned on the lights. The same macabre scene greeted him; a mannequin sprawled facedown across a desk, a hole beneath the shoulder with red paint simulating blood running down the figure's back.

He studied the wound. It was round, almost an inch in diameter. Round? What kind of instrument would leave a round hole? It was much too large for an ice pick.

He looked around the room. Along the outside wall of the living area was a window. Beneath it was the bed. A TV sat on a hutch against the opposite wall. He moved closer to the window and read the placard.

The investigation concluded that this window could not have been an exit for the killer for it could not be opened. Years of paint had sealed it closed.

Galloway studied the window. He attempted to open it, but as the placard stated, it was firmly sealed. He couldn't budge it. Outside the window, the moonlight illuminated the thick branches of an ancient pecan tree moving slowly with the breeze.

He paused in the kitchen doorway. His gaze swept around the small room to a table and two chairs against the outside wall. Above the tiny dining set was a small window beneath which another placard was fastened to the wall.

The only unlocked window in the apartment, but the size prevents an exit, and it is located on a sheer wall, offering no means of escape.

Galloway studied the window. It appeared to be around twelve to fourteen inches square. He opened it and stuck his head outside. He whistled. Sheer was right. The only projection in the outside wall was a decorative row of bricks projecting two inches out some three feet below. Ten feet to the left were limbs of the pecan tree he spotted from the window above the bed in the living area.

He studied the kitchen. Along the next wall, a set of cabinets surrounded an efficiency stove. In the corner stood the refrigerator. In the next corner was a dumbwaiter with a clock on the wall above the door. "I haven't seen a dumbwaiter in years," he muttered, leaning forward to read the placard next to the dumbwaiter door.

Upon initial investigation, the police believed the dumbwaiter to be the means of the killer's escape. On further investigation, they discovered that the door could not be closed from inside and both locks engaged.

The door is fastened by a self-locking spring latch plus a bar latch with automatic lock that prevents the bar from locking unless the spring were deliberately depressed, a task impossible to achieve from inside the dumbwaiter.

A balloon of cold air enveloped him. He ignored it, believing it to be coming from around the edges of the dumbwaiter door until he opened the door and a rush of warm air swept around him.

Frowning, he looked inside the dumbwaiter shaft. Below, a glow of lights from each floor cast thin beams of light through the dark shaft.

He stepped back in the room and closed the door and once again, cold air settled over him. He glanced around the room. "Must be a draft somewhere," he muttered, tinkering with the door locks, unable to find a means to refute the investigation's conclusion.

Opening the door again, he looked back inside. To his surprise, the top of the shaft was only six inches above the door opening for the waiter.

With a puzzled shake of his head, he closed the door and once again surveyed the room. The only unlocked exit was indeed the small window, which offered no means of escape even if someone could squirm through. He crossed the room to the window, but hesitated when he realized the air grew warmer as he approached the window.

Staying close to the wall, he circled the kitchen where the air remained warm. He extended his hand and eased forward, halting when his fingers encountered the cold air.

As best as he could discern, the balloon of cold air was five or six feet in diameter and centered in front of the dumb-waiter.

Galloway studied the walls and floors, looking for pinholes or cracks through which the cold air could pass. He had discovered the secret of the cold air in the bar and on the stairs, but he could discover no logical explanation for the puzzling occurrence by the dumbwaiter.

He knew it was one of Buster Collins' ghost ploys to enhance the mystery of the inn for his customers, but he couldn't figure this one out.

He removed the clock from the wall and carefully examined the wall over the dumbwaiter and the ceiling above, but he was unable to find Buster's secret. He shook his head. "However that con man did it, he's good."

He glanced up and down the hall when he closed the door behind him. He had the strangest feeling that he had almost discovered something important, but it had slipped away.

Having an hour to kill, Galloway lay in bed staring at the ceiling, going back over his theories and wondering how he could turn conjecture into fact.

As he replayed the means by which Carl Graves' killer exited the apartment, he dozed. In his dream, he was in the apartment. A man appeared and motioned him into the kitchen. As Galloway stepped through the door, the man vanished.

Galloway jerked awake. He shook his head. "Crazy dream," he muttered, staring at the ceiling, sorting and re-sorting his theories.

A frown played over his face. Suddenly alert, he stared at a tiny black dot on the ceiling. He studied it. On impulse, he stood up on the bed and inspected the dot.

A hole. A tiny hole.

Why? For what purpose? His first thought was Buster and his tricks.

He dragged a chair into the closet and pushed off the cover to the opening to the attic. He pulled himself up and peered into the darkness in the direction of his bedroom.

A tiny beam of white light shone through, casting a fuzzy glow on the roof. A narrow catwalk of planks spanned the ceiling joists. Holding to the overhead rafter, Galloway shuffled along the walk to the hole in the ceiling. He checked the adjoining room for a hole. None. In fact, none of the rooms in the wing except his had a hole in the ceiling.

"Someone must have been mighty interested in what I had to say," he whispered, peering into the darkness. "Mighty interested."

As he descended the stairs, he considered again the evidence in the case of George Sims. So far, it was circumstantial. About the only hard evidence he had was that the death was not murder, but manslaughter. The DA could decide if it was voluntary or involuntary.

Still, the man was dead; his wife was a widow; and his children, though grown, had lost their father.

Two hundred yards past Continental Delivery, a dirt road cut west through the pine and oak forest. Earlier in the day, Galloway had located a small clearing completely shielded from the road by thick vegetation.

Leaving his pickup in the clearing, he made his way along the dirt road to the highway, across which he darted. Staying close to the thick stands of wild azaleas and Chinese tallow, he hurried toward the gate, outside of which he crouched and waited.

Five minutes later, the security truck made its rounds and departed the warehouse parking lot. As it finally disappeared down the highway, Galloway raced across the parking lot. Deftly, he picked the front lock and stepped inside. He had not tripped any interior security alarms during his first visit so he kept his fingers crossed that Morgan had not added any since.

The only light in the warehouse was the suffused glow of the light through the opaque glass of the office. Remembering his earlier gaffe when he failed to lock the office door, Galloway deliberately locked it after gaining entrance to the office. He left the door open a crack so once he slipped out and closed it behind him, the lock would engage.

Moving quickly, he went directly to George Sims' desk and plopped down in his chair. Just as he reached for a drawer, he spotted a cassette recorder by the telephone on the edge of the desk. Galloway frowned and muttered. "Surely not. Not this easy."

He punched the play button. The first message was from a customer on Friday. Galloway rewound the tape. There were several routine messages on Wednesday until Sims picked up a call for David Morgan just after five o'clock. Apparently since Morgan was in Shreveport, Sims punched his extension. "Continental," he said.

"The shipment will be in Sunday night. What—"

Sims' voice broke in. "What shipment? Who is this?"

The caller quickly hung up.

Galloway knew the shipment to which the call referred— the drug shipment he had witnessed being unloaded Sunday night. The messages continued until a garrulous voice delivered the final, chilling one. "Sims. We know you heard the telephone call. If you don't want what Carl Graves got, then you keep your mouth shut."

For several seconds, Galloway stared at the recorder. Then

he realized his heart was thudding against his chest, and his breath was coming in short gasps. This was what Sims had been talking about. He stumbled to the drug deal; the dealer threatened him; and . . . and what? Galloway asked himself, remembering the video of Sims' death. In the next instant, he knew. Sims had not been murdered. The falling batten was indeed an effort to simply frighten the man, to warn him of the consequences if he squealed. But then fate stepped in.

A sharp pain struck Galloway in the back below his left shoulder, the same pain he had experienced in the séance. The same pain he had experienced two or three times since. He grimaced, and the recollection of the ghostly shadow he thought he saw on stage flashed through his mind. He shook his head. Impossible.

A creak from somewhere in the cavernous warehouse jarred him from his thoughts. Quickly, he ejected the cassette and slipped it in his pocket. He hesitated, then quickly removed the cassette and slid it in his sock. Even as he hastily secreted the cassette, he was asking himself why David Morgan had not removed the cassette.

Galloway opened the door slowly and peered into the shadows of the warehouse. Staying on the balls of his feet, he slipped into the darkness, heading for the front door. A flash of understanding froze him momentarily.

He hesitated by a pallet of boxes stacked head high. Now, he knew why Morgan had not taken the cassette. The only possible explanation was that Morgan had no idea of what was on it. Had he been responsible for the threatening call, then he would have immediately destroyed the cassette. As it was, the cassette remained in the recorder for a week.

"Hey, buddy. What do you think you're up to?"

The garrulous voice jerked Galloway back to the present. A shadowy figure stood in the darkness a few feet in front of him. He ducked his head and played for time. "Sorry, mister. Just trying to find a place for the night."

There was a moment of hesitation. "Well, you ain't gonna find it in here. How'd you get in anyway?"

Keeping his voice low and tremulous, Galloway replied. "The back door was unlocked. I, ah, I just walked in."

Suddenly, a beam of light blinded him.

"Hey. You're that detective guy," the figure shouted. "Elton, this—"

Galloway shoved the stack of boxes over on the smaller man. He spun toward the rear of the warehouse. He glimpsed another man, and then his head exploded.

The side of his face slammed into the cold concrete, and then a wave of blackness swept over him.

The next thing Galloway knew, voices were probing their way into the darkness surrounding him. He felt a warm liquid trickling down his forehead and dripping on the bridge of his nose.

"Jeez, Elton. I think you killed the guy."

Galloway remained motionless. A boot nudged him in the side. "Naw. He's just out cold."

"I don't know. Look at the blood. Must be a gallon."

Somewhere in the warehouse, a door opened, then slammed. "Cripes," muttered the garrulous voice. "Here's Morgan."

"Well, hello boys. You're here early. I like—hey, what's going on here? Who's that?"

"It's that detective dude, Mister Morgan. You know, the one who's been asking all them questions about Mister Sims."

"What's he doing here?"

"Snooping around. Me and Caleb got here a couple of minutes early. We heard a noise and found this guy."

Galloway felt hands rolling him onto his back. He remained limp, lifeless. A hand rested on his chest. "At least, he's alive," Morgan said, his voice only inches from Galloway's face. "Looks like you cracked open his skull."

Caleb spoke up. "I figure he was snooping around about this shipment."

Galloway recognized the garrulous voice on the recording. Caleb. He was the one who threatened Sims.

Morgan snorted. "How could he know about it? Nobody knew except me and the supplier. Did you search this guy?"

"No, sir."

"Do it."

Fingers rummaged his pockets. "What's all this?" Caleb asked, holding up a small leather case.

Morgan opened it. "Here. Shine the light here." The flashlight beam illumined a set of lock picks. With a grunt, Morgan snapped the case shut. "Anything else?"

"Just some change, a package of matches, and his wallet with three hundred bucks in it," Caleb said.

Elton grinned. "We can sure use that."

"Leave it alone. Put everything back. When they find him, if they find him, I don't want anything missing."

Caleb stuffed Galloway's property back in his pocket. "You wanting us to get rid of him, Mister Morgan?"

Morgan hesitated, searching for other options. "I don't see a choice. I don't know what he was looking for, but I can't afford to take a chance. Yeah. After we unload the truck, get rid of him. Take him out to Alligator Bayou."

"Yes, sir." Caleb chuckled. "This is one jam this dude won't get out of."

Morgan looked around at Caleb. "Huh? What do you mean, this is one jam he won't get out of?"

Taken aback by the question, Caleb stared at Morgan with wide eyes. "Do what? Huh?"

Morgan leaned forward. "I asked what you meant by that remark."

Caleb stammered.

Suddenly suspicious, Morgan cut his eyes to Elton. "You tell me, Elton. What's Caleb talking about?"

Elton dropped his gaze to the floor.

Caleb blurted out, "I didn't mean nothing, Mister Morgan. Honest."

Morgan kept his eyes fixed on Elton. "Don't play games with me, Elton. You'll be sorry."

Elton and Caleb exchanged furtive glances. In an apologetic voice, Elton replied, "Well, you see, Mister Morgan. We kind of wanted to run him out of the county before he could do much snooping. We tried a couple times to scare him, but it didn't work."

For several seconds, Morgan studied the two men. Between

the two, they couldn't manage enough brains to replace a refrigerator bulb. "I know you didn't do that on your own, Elton. Who put you up to it?" Morgan had an idea, but he wanted the answer.

"You tell him, Caleb."

"Well, you see, Mister Morgan. My girl, Elton's sister, works out at the Mystery Inn. Last Sunday at breakfast, she heard Bubba Collins hire this dude. She figured I might want to know, so she called me." He paused, his gaze fixed on the floor.

"So? Go on."

"So, I called Tennessee. He said you was gone. He didn't want nobody snooping, so he told us to go ahead and scare this guy off. We tried, twice, but it didn't work."

David Morgan stared at the two men for several seconds, doing his best to conceal the anger surging through his veins. He knew Caleb would run right back to Garcia and spill his guts. Better for Garcia to believe Morgan agreed with the decision.

"Well, boys. I wish I'd knowed about it, but you did the right thing."

The two men exchanged surprised looks.

"Really, Mister Morgan?" Elton gaped at him. "You ain't mad?"

"Naw. You boys did right. Tennessee did right. Now, tie this guy up and unload the truck. I got buyers coming in this morning around ten. You boys tape him up while I see if he got in the office."

Chapter Twenty-one

"He's plumb knocked out," Caleb said. "I don't see no sense in tying him up."

"We best. That's what Mister Morgan wants."

"Well, then, let's hurry up and do it."

Galloway feigned unconsciousness as Elton and Caleb duct-taped his ankles and then his wrists behind his back. "There," Caleb said. "That'll be good enough." They left him lying on the floor next to the pallet from which he had spilled the boxes.

The office door slammed. Morgan called out, "He tied up good?"

"Yes, sir, Mister Morgan. What about the office?"

"Nothing seems disturbed. Guess you boys stopped him before he got started. Now, let's unload that truck."

Galloway squinted through one eye as the footsteps retreated. He tried to open the other, but the caked blood had sealed it closed.

More times than he could count in his life, Galloway had found himself in serious situations. There might have been one or two more dicey than this one, but if there were, he couldn't remember them.

Galloway struggled to throw off the wooziness caused by the blow to his head. He could feel the throbbing just above his hairline. Sucking deep breaths of air into his lungs, he tried to pack his veins with fresh oxygen.

He wasted no time struggling against the tape. Instead, he scooted against the oak pallet and searched for protruding nails or rough edges from which shards of wood had splintered.

His fingers ran over the rough edges of the oak planks until they found a splintered edge. Squirming around so he could place his wrists on either side of the rough edge, he began sawing.

Keeping his eyes fixed on the far end of the warehouse, Galloway sawed at his bonds desperately as the men stacked cardboard boxes on a pallet. There was a logo on the boxes, but the distance was too far to make it out.

After what seemed like hours, the tape about his wrists parted. Before he could sit up, Morgan's voice echoed through the warehouse. "Okay, Elton. Close the door. That's it."

The truck door rattled down and clanged shut. Moments later, footsteps headed in his direction. "You just want to leave the goods out there, Mister Morgan, next to that pallet of seed corn?" Galloway recognized Caleb's guttural voice.

"Yeah. No sense in moving them around. They'll be out of here in a few hours."

The footsteps halted only a few feet from Galloway. "Hey, that guy's still unconscious."

Morgan snarled, "So what? Throw that bum on the dolly and dump him in the truck. I'm going home for a nap before our buyers arrive."

Rough hands tossed Galloway on the four-wheel dolly. He kept his eyes closed, but he could sense eyes on him as they rolled across the floor.

"You know what to do with him," Morgan called out as he closed the office door behind him. "Let me know before you leave."

Caleb grinned at Elton and cackled a cruel, cold laugh. "Yeah. We going to feed the 'gators tonight, ain't we, pardner?"

"He sure looks dead to me."

"Sure hope not. Won't be half the fun."

"Well, let's stop talking and get him loaded up."

Outside, they tossed Galloway in the pickup bed. Caleb spoke up. "Come on, Elton. Let's tell Morgan we're leaving."

Now was his chance, Galloway told himself, his brain racing. As soon as they went back inside, he'd make his break.

Elton spoke up. "You go tell him. I'll wait out here."

Galloway's hopes sank. I guess I go to plan B, he told himself, having absolutely no idea what plan B was.

Elton climbed in the pickup. As soon as the door slammed, Galloway opened his one eye and scanned the bed of the pickup. A few tools, a shovel, a jack and lug wrench, and a plastic container of gasoline with an accordion spigot.

He worked one arm loose of the frayed tape and scrubbed at the caked blood in his other eye, then jammed his hand in his pocket. A cruel grin played over his lips. Caleb and Elton were in for a surprise. And Morgan too if he had his way.

Turning his head so he could see through the rearview window, Galloway drew his knees to his chest and quickly unwound the tape around his ankles, taking care to leave it in place to give the appearance of being secure.

Then he lay back, and waited.

Five minutes later, Caleb returned. "Hoo, boy. Gimme a beer," he called out as he climbed into the passenger side of the pickup. "Let's us go out and have some fun now."

Galloway remained motionless until they turned down a dirt road that snaked through the dark forest. Through the rear window, he could see Caleb and Elton. He had to move fast, for as long as there were no overhead lights, he had an advantage. At night on a dark road, from inside a pickup cab the rear window acted like a mirror, reflecting the road ahead and making it nearly impossible to see into the bed of the pickup.

Kicking his feet free, Galloway squirmed out of his shirt and grabbed the gas can. He removed the spigot. The old Chevrolet pickup rattled and clanked over the sandy road, the noise hiding any that Galloway might make.

Galloway glanced into the cab of the pickup. Elton was staring down the road, and Caleb was chugging down a beer.

He soaked his shirt in gas, then slipped to the front of the bed and reached around the side of the cab to remove the cap to the gas tank. Quickly, he stuffed several inches of gasoline soaked shirt down the filler tube, then poured more gas over it after which he stuffed his gas-soaked handkerchief down the neck of the gas container, leaving a few inches dangling— a crude, but effective Molotov cocktail.

He knelt in front of the bed and pulled the pack of matches from his pocket. The wind swirling around the cab of the pickup whiffed the first one out. He broke off three or four and held them together while cupping his hands around the tip of the shirt.

The matches lit. The wind whipped at the flaring flame. He touched them to the soaked shirt, which erupted in a whoosh. Startled faces appeared in the back window.

Galloway touched the tip of the handkerchief to the flames, and as he leaped from the bed, he lobbed the gas can over the cab of the pickup. The flaming can slammed down on the hood of the pickup, instantly enveloping the front of the vehicle in flames.

The detective landed on his feet, but his momentum sent him tumbling to the ground, scraping the skin from one arm. He rolled over and watched as the old Chevrolet swerved from side to side. Both doors burst open, and arms and legs flailing, two figures leaped from the burning truck.

Moments later, a deafening explosion rocked the forest, and a brilliant fireball ballooned into the dark night. With a grin, Galloway hurried back up the road in the direction from which they had come. A few minutes later, a sheriff's car, overheads flashing, swept around a bend in the road. Galloway ducked into the underbrush as the cruiser roared past.

Back in his pickup, Galloway leaned on the steering wheel and stared out the window for several seconds, gathering his thoughts. He had been too busy in the warehouse and pickup trying to get himself out of a jam to analyze what he overheard while he feigned unconsciousness.

But now, he believed he knew just what had happened to George Sims. Unfortunately, he did not have the evidence to maintain an unbroken chain of responsibility back to David Morgan, but Galloway figured the drug dealer would be blown out of the saddle by the explosion when it took place— and it would.

And, he now believed he knew who had murdered Carl Graves five years earlier.

All he had to do now was come up with hard proof. He had to admit, those involved had managed to keep themselves pretty clean, but they had made a couple of mistakes. He realized he was stretching credibility with some of his hunches, but with luck, Galloway could take advantage of their mistakes.

He leaned to the side and laid his hand on his ankle to reassure himself that the cassette tape was still in his sock. A cruel grin twisted his lips. Now for David Morgan.

Shifting into gear, Galloway headed back to the warehouse.

The building was dark except for a single light in the office. Staying on the balls of his feet, Galloway hurried to the pallet of goods beside the pallet of seed corn. There were 30 boxes on the pallet, each about 12 by 15 inches square.

Deftly, he sliced the tape and opened a box. Inside was a bag of fine white powder, coke. He whistled softly. He tasted it, and shook his head in appreciation. "Good stuff." A sadistic grin curled his lips. "Someone's going to be mighty unhappy."

Working quickly, he dumped the contents of the boxes in a nearby trashcan and refilled the boxes with seed corn taken from the bags on the next pallet. He folded an empty bag over the seed so it wouldn't rattle, and then he jammed the empty seed corn bags on top of the goods in the trashcan.

To complete his deception, he rummaged through one of the shipping stations for a roll of brown tape, with which he then sealed each box.

With a grin, he stepped back and eyed his handiwork. "I sure wouldn't want to be in your shoes, Morgan."

Chapter Twenty-two

Galloway was waiting for Terp Howard when the sheriff returned from investigating the explosion and fire outside of town.

Terp jerked to a halt and stared at Galloway, noting the grimy undershirt and grease-stained slacks. "Kind of late to be working on your pickup, huh?"

Galloway grinned crookedly. "I wish." He gestured to the desk. "Sit. I've got a story for you."

In the next few minutes, Galloway quickly detailed his theories from the accidental death of George Sims to the murder of Carl Graves. He remained silent about the switch at the warehouse.

Terp Howard clicked his tongue when Galloway finished. "Well, you got some nice little ideas, but where's the proof?"

Galloway nodded to the recorder on the desk. "Listen to this."

Terp frowned. "What—"

"Just listen. I'll explain later."

Lighting a cigarette, the sheriff leaned back in his chair and stared at the recorder. He looked up at Galloway as Caleb threatened Sims. When the recording ended, he nodded. "That's Caleb's voice all right."

"That's the first step in hard evidence."

"You'll need a lot more than that. I can follow you on the Sims case. It makes sense, but Graves—I think you're really reaching there. No way the killer could have escaped through that small window. There was ice everywhere. It was January and we'd had us an ice storm a couple of days before."

"Ice storm?" Galloway's eyes lit. He leaned forward. "You say there was an ice storm?"

"Yeah."

With a grin, Galloway leaned back and nodded to the sheriff. "No, Terp, old friend. I'm not wrong. In fact, you've just handed me the murder weapon."

"I did what?"

"An icicle. The killer murdered Carl Graves with an icicle. You know, those big ones a foot long. Drive it in a 98.6-degree body, and within minutes, its melted."

Terp stared at Galloway for several seconds. He shook his head slowly. "Clever trick, but how are you going to prove it?"

With a sheepish grin, Galloway shrugged. "I've got an idea."

The sheriff tapped out his cigarette and nodded to the recorder. "How'd you get the tape?"

"For the record?"

"For the record."

Galloway cleared his throat. "Mrs. Sims gave me permission to look through her husband's things. I learned from Jennifer Pelt that Sims had a recorder on his telephone, so I simply removed the tape."

Terp arched an eyebrow. "Now, off the record."

With a sheepish grin, Galloway said, "I was afraid you were going to ask that." He paused a moment, then quickly filled in the missing information including setting the pickup on fire.

Leaning back in his chair, Terp shook his head and grinned. "I wondered just how all that happened. Elton and Caleb was mighty vague. I couldn't figure a lighted cigarette dropped in the floorboard could cause a fire like that."

"They give any reason for being out there?"

Terp chuckled. "Caleb claims he was going to do some repairs to their fish camp on the Sabine."

"You're kidding. He expected you to believe that?"

"You ought to know by now that they're not the brightest lights on the block."

Galloway glanced at his watch. "In a few hours, Morgan will be moving his goods."

"I can't stop them. I've got no probable cause."

A sly grin played over Galloway's face. "If things go like I think, you won't need it. Morgan will be coming here to you."

Terp frowned.

Galloway held up his hand. "I'll explain later. In the meantime, let's get Caleb in here." He pointed to the cassette. "Let's hear his explanation for this."

Terp arched an eyebrow. "You know, I got an idea about how we might just prompt him to talk." He leaned forward. "Now, listen. Here's what we'll do."

When Deputy Brocklin returned with Caleb Worster, the front office was empty. Brock pointed to a chair. "Have a seat there, Caleb. I'll tell Terp you're here."

Sullen, Caleb grunted, "I figured he got everything he needed about the fire a while ago."

Brock shrugged. "I don't know from nothing." He knocked on the door to the sheriff's office, then opened it slightly and stuck his head inside.

Caleb watched warily.

Brock pulled back, leaving the door open a few inches. "Yes, sir, Sheriff." He turned back to Caleb. "Sheriff will be right out. Go ahead and smoke if you want. I've got to go out to the cruiser."

As soon as Brock disappeared outside, Caleb edged closer to the door. He slumped lazily in a chair and lit a cigarette, but his attention was on the voices coming through the open door. Suddenly, he froze when he heard his name. "That's right. Caleb Worster. We think he's probably the number two man in the organization. We have pretty firm proof that he ordered at least one murder, was present in two additional attempts, and we have a recording of felony threats. That's why we want you FBI boys to come in and give us a hand."

Caleb's heart leaped into his throat. FBI? Number two

man? Murder? Not me, he told himself. They can't be talking about me. They got everything all wrong.

He cut his eyes toward the front door. He couldn't run. Brock was just outside. Even if he did escape, they'd be looking for him.

A voice cut into his thoughts, startling him. "Hello, Caleb."

Caleb jumped. He looked up to see the sheriff standing in the doorway. "Huh? What? Oh, hey, Sheriff."

Terp indicated Galloway. "I think you know this gentleman."

Remaining seated, Caleb played dumb. "I don't think so."

Galloway grinned amicably. "Sure you do, Caleb. Why just a couple of hours ago, you and your buddy, Elton, were taking me up to your fishing camp. Unfortunately, your truck caught on fire."

Caleb glanced nervously at Terp. "You're right about the fire, but I don't know nothing about taking you fishing." He looked straight into Galloway's eyes, daring him to disagree.

With a chuckle, Galloway continued. "Say what you want, Caleb. We know you're responsible for the death of George Sims, and we know you're a dealer."

He shook his head emphatically. "You don't know no such thing."

"No? Well, Caleb, let me tell you just what we do know. We know Elton's sister, Elisha, told you that Bubba Collins had hired me to find evidence to prove Mary Calvin did not kill Sims; we know you and Elton told Tennessee Garcia, and he ordered you to frighten me off. And we know you use Continental Delivery for your drug deals whenever David Morgan is gone." Galloway glanced at Terp. "Caleb probably figures Morgan will be blamed."

Caleb's forehead wrinkled in a frown. "What do you mean when Morgan's gone?"

Galloway shrugged. "Just what I said. You're using a legitimate business for drug deals. Morgan's an honest man, and you and your bunch are taking advantage of him."

Caleb's mouth flapped once or twice, but no words came out. His gaze darted around the room, and he shook his head. "You got it wrong. That ain't the way it is."

"Oh? Just how is it then?"

Caleb opened his mouth, then closed it. He shook his head. "You can't prove nothing."

Galloway pulled the cassette tape from his pocket. "No? You want to hear the threat you made to George Sims last Thursday?"

"I didn't make no threats."

"You didn't tell him that if he opened his mouth, he'd get the same thing Carl Graves got?"

Caleb shook his head. "I didn't say nothing like that."

"No." Galloway inserted the cassette in the recorder. "Let's hear just what you did say."

Galloway turned on the recorder. "What do you want to bet, Sheriff, that this will solve two murders for you?"

When Caleb Worster heard George Sims' voice, he jumped to his feet. "No!" Wild-eyed, he hurled his chair at the two men. He broke for the door, jerking it open and running over Deputy Brocklin, sending him tumbling to the ground.

He jumped in Brock's cruiser in a desperate effort to escape. Fortunately, at three o'clock in the morning traffic was non-existent in Towson, so Caleb Worster only jeopardized his own life as he swept through town at 80 miles an hour.

Terp and Galloway were on his tail in the sheriff's cruiser. "That crazy idiot," the sheriff muttered. His jaw set, his fingers tight about the wheel, he added, "Well, Galloway. I'd say we broke him down."

"For all the good it's doing us right now. Faster."

Ahead, the cruiser whipped off the highway down a dirt road.

"This is the same one they took me earlier."

"He's heading for his fish camp. He has a boat there."

"Won't the Louisiana law pick him up on the other side?"

Terp shook his head. "He won't cross the river. Once he gets back in these sloughs and woods, he can lose himself forever."

"Then floorboard this thing."

Ahead, the brake lights of the cruiser flashed.

"He's there."

Caleb leaped out and dashed down a trail.

"Look out," Terp shouted. "He left the car in gear." He slammed on the brakes as the driverless cruiser backed toward them.

Just before the two cruisers collided, Galloway leaped from the sheriff's cruiser and raced after the smaller man disappearing into the darkness of the swamp.

The moonlight cast patches of bluish white on the ground. Suddenly, running footsteps on wood echoed through the darkness. Moments later, Galloway reached the dock that stretched into the river.

From the shadows at the end of the dock came the sounds of an outboard motor being cranked.

He sprinted down the dock. Abruptly, the motor roared to life. Caleb's gleeful voice echoed above the roar. "Better luck next time, sucke—"

A thump, the rip of splitting wood, and a terrified scream followed by a loud splash cut off Caleb Worster's cry of triumph.

In the pale starlight, Galloway saw that in his haste, Caleb had cast off the bow line, but overlooked the second line mooring the stern of his boat. When the speeding boat hit the end of the rope, the impact ripped the transom and motor off.

For several moments, the only sounds from the darkness were the gurgling of the sinking boat. Then frightened screams cut through the night. "Help! Help!"

Terp slid to a halt behind Galloway and shouted, "Swim, Caleb! Swim for all you're worth!"

Caleb swam frantically.

Terp peered closely into the dark waters surrounding the frightened man, searching for the telltale wakes of hungry alligators.

Galloway shouted. "Terp! Behind him. A big wake. Shoot!"

"Where? Where?"

"Behind him. Off to the left." Galloway pointed at a shadow throwing off a wake.

Terp aimed at the shadow and fired. A geyser of water erupted into the air just in front of the shadow.

Caleb flailed at the water and cried out. "Help, Sheriff! Help me!"

"Faster, Caleb! Faster," Galloway shouted, leaning forward and waving to the frantic man.

Terp fired again. The .357 boomed, and water exploded behind Caleb. A loud splash followed the echo of the .357 as the alligator whipped the water with his tail, swerving from the impact of the slug in the water.

"Hurry, Caleb," Terp shouted, firing once again.

By now, the flailing, sobbing man was less than 20 feet from the dock. Galloway dropped to his knees and extended his hand, hooking his other arm around a pier so he wouldn't be pulled into the water. "Here, Caleb. Here. Grab my hand."

Less than 10 feet from the dock, Caleb swam through a patch of light. His eyes were wide with fear. He grabbed at Galloway's hand. Their fingers touched, and then, with a sudden rush, the alligator struck.

The terror-stricken man managed a horrific shriek before he was spun under water, which churned into froth as the alligator continued rolling with his prey firmly locked in his jaws.

Caleb managed another cry before the waters closed over his head for the final time.

Cursing, Terp emptied his magnum and fumbled to extract extra cartridges from his belt. Before he could reload, two more alligators lunged forward.

All they found later was Caleb's Houston Astros cap floating on the surface of the muddy water.

Terp left one of his deputies and the doctor to watch the scene and retrieve any parts of Caleb that might float to the surface.

Chapter Twenty-three

Terp shook his head. "I hope you know what you're doing, Galloway. Elton isn't real smart, but he isn't stupid."

"That's what I'm counting on. I want him to give you enough probable cause to pull his sister in."

"I understand what you have, but it seems mighty shaky to me."

"I don't think so."

A knock at the door interrupted them. Deputy Collins stuck his head inside. "Elton's here, Sheriff."

Elton Brister looked nervously from the sheriff to Galloway. "What's going on, Sheriff? Why'd you have Collins bring me in this early?"

Terp sighed. "Well, Elton, I don't suppose you heard about Caleb."

"Caleb?" He glanced suspiciously at Galloway, then back at Terp. "What about Caleb."

Terp opened his desk drawer and tossed the wet cap on the desk in front of Elton. Water pooled on the desk. "This is all that's left of old Caleb. 'Gators got him down at your fish camp."

Elton's eyes bulged. He stared in disbelief before a faint grin flickered across his face. "You're pulling my leg, Terp. What's really going on?"

"I'll tell you, Elton," Terp replied. "But first, I want to give you your rights."

With a glassy look in his eyes, Elton stood silently while Terp Mirandaed him, after which the confused man agreed he understood his rights.

Then Galloway spoke up. "It's the truth about Caleb, Elton. Deputy Brocklin and the doctor are still out there, seeing what they can retrieve."

The disbelief faded into a grimace. "Caleb? But, w-what happened?"

"Seems like Caleb got himself mixed up in some serious stuff around here, Elton. He was trying to escape arrest."

Elton's expression grew guarded. "Serious stuff? What are you talking about, Sheriff?"

"I'll tell you, Elton," Galloway said. "You see, we know your sister told you and Caleb that Buster Collins out at the Mystery Inn hired me. Caleb told Tennessee Garcia who then ordered you boys to run me out of the country."

"That ain't so." Elton glared at Galloway belligerently.

Ignoring the denial, Galloway continued. "Had to be. When I returned to the inn, a message in lipstick was on my mirror telling me to mind my own business. Your sister is the only one who could have put it there. She works at the inn, so no one would pay any attention to where she went."

Elton tried to smirk. "That's a bunch of bull."

"Think so, huh? You might be interested in knowing that I have me a nice little bumper in the back of my pickup. A pipe bumper. It was torn off an '84 Chevy pickup which fired shots at my truck. I got me a sneaking feeling that the sheriff here will be able to match it to your pickup."

Elton's face paled. He glanced at the sheriff, then back to Galloway, who continued. "And we have proof Caleb called George Sims and threatened him." He changed topics. "What kind of cigarettes does your sister smoke?"

"Huh?"

Terp spoke up. "You heard him. What kind of cigarette does Elisha smoke?"

"Kools. So what?"

Terp and Galloway nodded at each other, and Galloway

continued. "Because I can prove your sister was standing just outside the stage door during the play on Saturday night." He fished a plastic bag with two cigarette butts from his shirt pocket. "These are your sister's, and that's her lipstick."

Elton licked his lips. "You can't prove that. Besides, she was working the bar that night."

Galloway shook his head at Terp and hooked a thumb toward Elton. "Is he always this dense?"

"I told you there were brighter bulbs on the tree."

Elton frowned, unable to follow the exchange between Terp and Galloway, who grew serious. "Your sister did not work that night. She never showed. Myrt worked Elisha's shift."

"Okay, so she didn't work. So what?"

Terp leaned forward. "So, we figure she had a hand in Sims' murder, and that you and Caleb knew about it."

Before Elton could protest, Galloway said, "You ever hear of DNA, Elton?"

Clearly puzzled, Elton looked at Galloway. "Huh?"

Galloway held up the plastic bag. "There's a method that can tell exactly who smoked this cigarette." He pointed to the dark lipstick. "You see, Elton. When Elisha touched her lips to this cigarette, she left the lipstick, and the lipstick contains moisture from her lips. No two people are alike. And I imagine the lipstick on the cigarette butts will match that on the mirror and with your sister."

Elton looked at Terp, who nodded. "He's telling you the truth."

Elton tried to sort the myriad of questions ricocheting around in his head. Galloway saw the confusion in the younger man's eyes.

"Let me tell you what happened, Elton. You, Caleb, Garcia, and Morgan have been dealing coke, Ecstasy, and other pills. The deliveries come in a truck from Express Unlimited."

Elton stared at Galloway in surprise. He shrugged. "We got trucks from all over."

"I know, but how many of them have false floors?"

Elton's jaw hit the floor. Galloway continued. "Morgan's paying Garcia to look the other way, just like Carl Graves did five years ago. But he's greedy, too greedy. That's why after you and Caleb unloaded the first shipment, Morgan called you back to help unload the goods he didn't want Garcia to know about. If Garcia doesn't know about them, Morgan doesn't have to pay him off."

Sweat beaded on Elton's broad forehead. "You ain't got no proof."

"But I have, Elton. I have enough to put you away for murder one if you don't start cooperating."

Elton leaned forward, resting his elbows on his knees and staring at the floor.

"He's telling you the truth, Elton," Terp said. "Now, I've known you a bunch of years. You never was real smart, but you best ought to try to help yourself. You don't, you might not have another chance."

Elton kept his head bowed and remained silent.

Galloway spoke softly. "Here's what I figured happened, Elton. Caleb called for Morgan. Sims picked up the phone, and Caleb told him the shipment would be in Sunday. Caleb realized it was Sims he talked to, not Morgan, so he called back and threatened him." Galloway paused. "Right so far?"

Elton remained silent, staring at the floor.

"Saturday night before the play, Elisha or you or maybe even Caleb slipped backstage and rewound the batten rope around the pin. Elisha skipped her shift and waited just outside the door to the stage. While she waited, she smoked two cigarettes before she slipped inside. The side curtains kept the actors from spotting her. After that, it was simply a matter of reaching around the end of the curtain and slipping the pin from the rail. We know you didn't mean to kill Sims. You just wanted to scare him."

Elton raised his head and Galloway saw the desperation in his eyes.

"If you think Morgan or Garcia will help you, think again. You remember that pallet loaded with goods you unloaded a few hours ago? Well, I dumped the goods and filled the boxes with seed corn. What do you think will happen when the buyers open the boxes?"

Unable to hide his astonishment, he gaped at Galloway. "You—you what?"

"You heard me."

"But-but Morgan said them goods were worth over a hundred thousand."

From the corner of his eye, Galloway saw Terp shake his head at Elton's complete disintegration of any façade of innocence. With a shrug, Galloway remarked, "Doesn't surprise me. Who do you think Morgan will figure pulled the doublecross, that is, if they let him live that long."

Elton's eyes grew wide as pie plates. He looked at Terp frantically. "You got to tell them I had nothing to do with that, Sheriff."

Terp snorted. "I got to do nothing except die and pay taxes, Elton."

"If Morgan spills the truth first, you're left out in the cold, Elton," Galloway said, prodding the frightened man.

Swallowing hard, Elton glanced over his shoulder. He dragged his hand over his lips. Abruptly, he nodded. "Yeah. That's what happened. But we didn't mean to kill Sims. They said he just stumbled under the stage lights. We was just meaning to scare him. He just fell under the lights hisself."

An hour later, two police cruisers parked beside the red Viper at Continental Delivery. Terp and Galloway climbed from one, and Deputy Brocklin from the other.

Morgan covered his surprise when he saw Galloway. "What can I do for you, Sheriff?"

"It isn't so much what you can do for us, Morgan," Galloway said. "It's more likely we can help you."

Morgan arched an eyebrow. "I don't understand."

"First, you should know that Caleb's dead. The 'gators got him."

"What?" Morgan frowned at Terp.

The sheriff nodded.

Gesturing to the empty space on the floor where the pallet of drugs had sat, Galloway said, "I see you moved your goods."

Instantly wary, he replied, "What goods? What do you mean?"

"I know you'll just deny any accusations, Morgan, so I'll come right out and tell you that after your boys bungled their orders to dump me in Alligator Bayou, I came back here, and while you were home taking a nap, I dumped the goods and replaced them with seed corn from the pallet next to them."

Morgan looked like he'd been struck between the eyes with a sledgehammer, but he tried to hide his confusion. "What goods? I don't know what you're talking about."

"The boxes you unloaded and stacked on the pallet right there," Galloway replied, pointing to the empty space.

"I still don't know what you're talking about." Morgan looked at Terp. "He's crazy, Sheriff."

Galloway pointed to a trashcan next to a large door. "Take a look over there, Brock. Tell us what you find."

Brocklin looked in the can. "Just some empty seed bags."

"Under the bags."

Brocklin lifted the paper and whistled in disbelief. "You ain't going to believe this, Sheriff, but this trash can is plumb full of happy powder."

Morgan rolled his eyes. "Nice try, Brock."

The deputy picked up a handful and poured it back into the trashcan.

Morgan's eyes bulged. "What? It can't be." He raced to the can. He stared into it. His face paled. He closed his eyes and swallowed hard. "I'm dead."

Terp indicated the drugs. "That yours, Morgan?"

For a moment Morgan hesitated, indecision filling his eyes.

Galloway said. "Two choices. Deny the goods, and you walk out of here—for a day or so. Then you'll end up like Caleb. Or admit the goods are yours and go to jail. At least, you'll be alive."

Morgan glared murderously at Galloway and muttered a curse.

Chapter Twenty-four

Sipping hot coffee, Galloway nodded to the cellblock overhead. "Looks like you're getting a full complement of prisoners, Terp."

"Looks that way. I imagine Morgan and Elton are glad to be up there." He shook his head. "Can't say as much for Elisha. She's a tough one. Folks say she shoulda been the man and Elton the woman in that family."

"Mary Calvin was happy though."

"Yeah." The sheriff leaned back and grinned at Galloway. "That was the good part of it, turning her loose."

"Sure you won't have any trouble? There was no legal order to free her."

Terp shook his head. "Still the city boy, aren't you? Out here, we cut through the nonsense. A release will be along. Don't worry about that. By the way, did you say anything to her about her father?"

Galloway shook his head. "Why?"

"Her husband told her about Buster." He sipped his coffee. "Forget about her. You need to worry about tonight. What if they don't show?"

Rising, Galloway stretched his arms and groaned. "I'm beat. Don't worry. They'll show. Some of them have been searching for Graves' money for five years." He shook his head. "They'll show."

"You telling me, you know where the money is?"

"No idea, but they don't know that."

Terp laughed. "Don't you think you're stretching the melodrama a little by meeting at midnight?"

Galloway's grin grew wider. "Probably. But, that's when the spooks come out. With luck, we'll have our own little ghost tonight."

Back at the inn, Galloway showered and tried to grab a couple of hours' sleep. He dreamed, and in his dream he was back in the apartment, and the same man gestured him into the kitchen. Galloway tried to run after the man so he wouldn't escape this time, but his feet were mired in the floor. When he did reached the kitchen door, the man, instead of simply vanishing as in the previous dream, vanished into the clock above the dumbwaiter.

He jerked awake, a wild and crazy thought in his head. "Do you think . . ." His voice trailed off. Quickly, he climbed from bed and hurriedly dressed. He muttered to himself as he headed upstairs.

Galloway was right. Everyone showed up for the midnight tour of the stage and of the murder apartment. In addition to the cast members, diminutive Jennifer Pelt, Sara Hoffpauir, the stockbroker Aaron Lyman, Ola Mae Sims Wilkerson, and Buster Collins were in attendance.

They met in the bar. Sheriff Terp Howard closed the door and nodded to Galloway. "It's your show."

The expressions on their faces were a mixture of curiosity and apprehension. Sean Ross, the director of the play, rose from his chair. "What's this all about, Galloway?"

"Fair question, Mister Ross. I questioned everyone in this room about the death of George Sims. For your information, and to put you minds to rest, none of the information I learned about any of you goes beyond me or your sheriff except for the guilty party." He noticed the relief in some eyes, the sharpening of awareness in others. "I can tell you that none of you were responsible for the death of George Sims. Those responsible are in jail at this time."

A gasp of astonishment swept around the room. Ola Mae Sims Wilkerson hiccupped. "Wh-who did it?"

Galloway shook his head. "That's for the sheriff to say. The reason I have all of you here is to show you how Sims was killed, and then take you to the apartment on the third floor to point out the location of the quarter million Carl Graves hid."

An excited murmur spread through the small group.

Terp opened the hall door leading to the stage. Galloway led the way. Once on the stage, he demonstrated how the rope was wound around the pin, and just how easily and silently the perpetrator could slip behind the side curtain and surreptitiously remove the pin from the rail. "The death was unintentional. The falling stage lights were meant to frighten Sims, but for some reason, he stumbled just as the light batten fell." He said nothing about the shadow he himself had seen.

Mary Calvin cleared her throat. "You mean, it was just a horrible accident?" Disbelief filled her voice.

Galloway hesitated, then nodded. "Yes." After another pause, Galloway gestured to the third floor. "Now for what everyone has been searching the last five years."

After the small group crowded into the apartment, Terp closed the door and took his place in front of it. He nodded to Galloway.

"What made Sims' death so confusing was the way it was intertwined with the death of Carl Graves," Galloway began.

Buster Collins interrupted. "But where's the money, Galloway?"

Galloway grinned. "I don't know how you missed it, Buster. With all the ghost gimmicks you've planted around the inn, you did everything except walk on it. It's here, in the kitchen."

To his surprise, the pocket of cold air had vanished. It had been present earlier, but now, it had disappeared. Galloway glanced around, deciding the number of people crowding into the kitchen had blocked the hidden draft, causing the pocket to dissipate.

He stopped at the dumbwaiter door. "I know many of you

have searched the inn for the alleged cash. In fact, I attribute many of the sounds from the attic not to ghosts, like Buster here wants his customers to think, but to those looking for the money."

Buster shrugged and grinned. "What about the money?"

The others joined in.

"First," Galloway said, eyeing Buster, "the standard rate for a finder's fee is twenty-five percent."

The owner of the inn gulped and nodded. "Good enough."

Galloway removed the clock from above the dumbwaiter, revealing a hole in the wall. "I did that earlier to make sure I was right."

"Were you? Were you?" As one, the small group stepped forward.

Using his knife, Galloway carved a foot-wide square in the sheetrock and popped it out. Beyond the opening was a leather satchel. He pulled it out and opened it.

As they stared at the money, Galloway continued. "Now Graves' gambling addiction had dug a deep hole with some pretty heavy men." He grinned at Sarah Hoffpauir. "Graves claimed he was saving the money for his old age. Some say he should have used it to pay off his debts, but contrary to local belief, he was not murdered because of his gambling debts."

A sharp intake of breath greeted his announcement.

Sara Hoffpauir shook her head. "Then, why was he killed, Mister Galloway?"

Galloway studied each face before him. "Revenge."

Buster Collins coughed. "Revenge? For what?"

Galloway slid his gaze around the group and focused on a single individual. "You want to tell them why, Ms. Pelt?"

With a collective gasp, the group turned and stared at Jennifer Pelt whose eyes turned hard and cold. "I don't know what you're talking about, Galloway."

"Oh, yes, you do. You used an icicle to murder Carl Graves because you believed he was responsible for the death of your sister, Carol Ann Moses, eight years ago."

"That's absurd. I'll admit, Carl Graves got what he deserved, but I didn't kill him. Even if I had, I wouldn't have used an icicle."

"That was a nice touch. When it melted, there was no weapon, no prints, no DNA. Yeah, that was a real smooth touch."

"You're crazy."

"You stabbed him, locked the door, and slipped out the window above the table."

She shook her head adamantly. "You're insane."

Galloway ignored her protest. "What really makes this interesting is that you and Sims had an affair."

"So? He had several affairs. A lot of men have affairs."

"With two sisters?"

Jennifer Pelt's eyebrows knit in puzzlement. "What are you talking about?"

Galloway held his breath, hoping she would take the bait. "You and your sister."

She snorted. "You're crazy. George and I had an affair, but he didn't have one with my sister. It was Graves."

Shaking his head, Galloway asked, "How did you know that? She tell you?"

"No." Pelt shook her head emphatically. "George did. Everyone knew what a hustler Carl was. When he learned that my sister was pregnant, he dumped her. She killed herself because of him."

Galloway's next words hit her squarely between the eyes. "George Sims lied to you, Ms. Pelt. He had the affair with your sister. She was pregnant with his child, and she killed herself because of him."

She stared at him, her eyes wide with incredulous disbelief.

Before she could reply, he handed her a sheet of paper. "The sheriff has eyewitnesses who have sworn your sister visited the Purple Sleeve Nightclub in Houston with Sims. Here is an arrest record showing that the two of them were arrested when the dive was busted."

The diminutive woman's hand trembled as she read the arrest record. She shook her head and glared at Galloway, tears brimming her eyes. "This is a lie. All a lie." Desperation edged her words.

Galloway shook his head. "No. And you know it isn't. You gave yourself away when you claimed you didn't see Graves the day of his death."

"I didn't. It was the day before."

"No. You said when you saw him, he was trying to straighten out one of the company accounts."

She nodded emphatically, her gaze shifting around the room nervously. "That's right."

"You even knew the name of the account. What was it, Wholesale Supplies, out of Shreveport?"

"Yes."

Galloway glanced at Terp who shook his head slowly. The sheriff knew as well as Galloway that Jennifer felt had just confessed. "That was impossible. Morgan handed Graves the books thirty minutes before he was found dead. The only way you could have known about those books is if you were there that day."

Her face paled momentarily, and then she glared fiercely at Galloway. She clenched her teeth. "You—you—"

With a chilling scream, she hurled her purse at Galloway and in a burst of surprising strength, slung Sara Hoffpauir to the floor, causing several of the group to stumble.

In the next instant, Pelt ripped the small window open, and squirted through.

Galloway raced to the window. He shot out his hand and grabbed her wrist. "Don't try it!" he shouted.

With a guttural cry, she tore her arm free of his grasp and leaped for the oak limb. In the bright moonlight, Galloway made out her slender outline as she stretched for the limb.

He heard the slap of her hands, and a spontaneous grunt as she swung under the limb. Suddenly, a sharp crack broke the silence, and a terrified scream echoed through the night as the limb snapped in two, sending Pelt plummeting to the ground.

Galloway shouted over his shoulder. "Terp! She fell!"

The shadows cast by the leaves and limbs of the oak obscured his vision. He heard branches breaking, sharp exclamations as she bounced from limb to limb, and finally a dull thump.

To his amazement, a shadowy figure raced from beneath the tree. "Terp. She's getting away. Hurry. Get down there. I'll try to watch from here."

The nebulous shadow ghosted across the lawn and blended into the bed of roses along one side of the parking lot.

Moments later, Terp leaped from the porch, flashlight in hand.

"The parking lot," Galloway shouted. "By the roses."

The sheriff slowed as he approached the rose bed, the beam of his light darting back and forth along the length of the bed. "She isn't here."

Muttering a curse, Galloway bounded down the stairs. While Hoffpauir and Mary Calvin watched from the porch, the others joined the search.

Five minutes later, Don Shahan called out, "Here she is. Over here. Behind the tool shed. There's blood everywhere."

Chapter Twenty-five

T erp knelt by the prostrate woman, his fingers on her right carotid. The left had a ragged gash in it. He laid his hand on her heart and shook his head. "She's dead." He focused the beam on her ripped carotid. "She must have torn it open on one of the branches when she fell."

After the corpse had been taken away, the small group retired to the bar. "I could use a stiff bracer," Sean Ross said.

Buster Collins arched an eyebrow at Terp. "No charge, folks. It's after hours, and I'm staying legit."

Terp chuckled. "Break it out, Buster. We'll forget the curfew. We're all friends here." He sat across the table from Galloway. "Well, you haven't lost your touch. I was even impressed. I figured you had too many gaps to fit it all together."

Galloway agreed. "There were some. And all this haunting business didn't help. Sims was an accident. The entire cast saw him stumble under the batten. It was just one of those freak things."

"Yes," Mary Calvin said. "But it led to the killer of Carl Graves. How did you figure it was Jennifer?"

"It couldn't have been anyone else. Her sister committed suicide and reliable sources said George Sims was her lover." He exchanged a knowing look with Don Shahan and continued. "Sims put the blame for the sister's death on Graves."

"He must have felt terrible when Carl was killed?"

"We'll never know. One thing I'll say for Pelt, she was clever. In addition to being an acrobat in the circus, she was double-jointed. As part of her Rubber Woman routine, she closed herself in a suitcase. As soon as I heard that, I knew she could have slipped out the window. From there to the nearest limb was no problem."

Mary Calvin cleared her throat. "Mister Galloway. What will happen to those who killed George?"

Galloway deferred to the sheriff. "Be up to the DA, Mary," Terp said. "Manslaughter. Involuntary maybe."

"I'm so sorry, but I want to thank you for helping me, Mister Galloway. My husband and children and I will never forget you."

Galloway nodded to Collins. "Thank him. He's the one who insisted you were innocent."

She smiled gently up at Buster Collins. "My husband believes you're my father."

Collins glanced at Galloway who simply arched an eyebrow as if to say the ball was in his court now. He looked back at Mary Calvin. "I was afraid to tell you ... afraid that ..." She took his hand in hers. Tears filled her eyes. "Thank you. Thank you for believing in me—Father."

After loading his Silverado for the trip back to Houston, Galloway stopped in Buster Collins' office. Beaming, Collins grinned up at him and reached for his checkbook. "You did all I asked for, Galloway, and more. What more can I give you?"

"I've got enough. Now, let's talk about the finder's fee. I want you to give it to the sheriff's department. Terp and the boys can use it."

Buster opened a bottom drawer in his desk and retrieved a bottle of Johnny Walker Red. "Join me, Galloway. The sun's over the yardarm somewhere. We'll seal it with a drink."

"Why not? What about your share?"

Collins' grin grew wider. "The kids. I'd like to help the kids get their own business." He gestured to the office. "I'd love for them to come here and help run this place, but I ain't pushing no one. I'm just grateful for what I have—for what you gave me." Tears brimmed his eyes, and he extended his hand. "Thanks."

Galloway took his hand. "No problem." He downed the drink, and headed for the door.

Collins held up the bottle. "Another?"

"No. Thanks. One's enough." Galloway paused at the door and looked back. "By the way, those little ghost tricks of yours are slick."

He laughed. "You like them, huh? What about the cold air that comes from the bar?"

"That had me going. And the ones on the stairs. It took me a while to find them."

Collins chuckled again. "Marketing, Galloway. Marketing."

"But, I'm puzzled. The only one I couldn't find was in the apartment, in the wall by the dumbwaiter. How did you get the cold air there?"

Collins frowned. "In the apartment? Upstairs?" He shook his head. "I didn't do anything to that one."

Galloway stared at him in disbelief. Then he remembered the shadow he thought he had seen behind George Sims, the shadow and the ball of light.

Was it possible?

"You didn't rig any ghost tricks up there? What about in the theater?"

He shook his head. "No. Not a one."

Galloway whistled softly and nodded to the bottle of Johnny Walker Red. "Maybe I will take that second drink."